The Deadly Doves

By the same author

Blood on the Saddle
The Comanche's Ghost
Blood Pass
The West Witch
Wanted
Ghost-Town Duel
The Gallows Ghost
The Widow Maker
Guns of the Past
Palomita
The Last Draw

The Deadly Doves

LANCE HOWARD

A Black Horse Western

ROBERT HALE · LONDON

© Howard Hopkins 1999
First published in Great Britain 1999

ISBN 0 7090 6454 3

Robert Hale Limited
Clerkenwell House
Clerkenwell Green
London EC1R 0HT

The right of Howard Hopkins to be identified as
author of this work has been asserted by him
in accordance with the Copyright, Designs and
Patents Act 1988.

Photoset in North Wales by
Derek Doyle & Associates, Mold, Flintshire.
Printed and bound in Great Britain by
WBC Book Manufacturers Limited, Bridgend.

ONE

Whip Foley let out a disgusted grunt and threw down his losing hand. The cowboy sitting across from him grinned and bellowed a laugh. The laugh sent irritation skittering through Whip's nerves and heat rushing into his face. Galldamn, he was plumb tired of losing and had durn few of his thirty greenbacks pay from the temporary job – temporary until Lady Luck did a dosi-do and flashed her golden smile his way – he'd signed on to at the Double H compound breaking horseflesh burning holes in his britches.

Not that he wasn't a hell of a fine bronc snapper – ride 'em once or put 'em in a family mind – but, Judas H. Priest, he couldn't rightly cotton to working for a living when he fancied himself one of them vest-spruced, silver-tongued card sharps. Except Lady Luck hadn't so much as shown a glimpse of her pearly whites for more weeks than he could recollect and if he didn't break horseflesh he didn't eat.

Whip's real name was Waldo Foley. His mother, a no-good saloon whore who, when he was nine, had run off with a half-breed flesh peddler, always called him Wally, which he detested and changed the moment the no-good tramp left. A few kids at the orphanage had saddled him with 'walleye' a-cause his eyes were a little bigger than his sockets wanted to accommodate and made him look like one of them ugly little Chinese dogs he'd seen once.

At forty-five, Whip was beginning to run to seed. Gray streaks highlighted lusterless black, stringy hair that fell to one side of his forehead while a roll of fat stretched his shirt over his belt line. His clothing reeked of horse lather, sweat and dung, and he reckoned soon as his luck turned he'd buy himself one of them fancy stinks that cost two dollars a bottle and take a galldamn bath in it.

'Not your night, gent.' The cowboy across from him scooped up the pile of greenbacks and silver dollars.

'Ain't never my night lately,' Whip said with a sneer and stood, grabbing his hat and the nearly empty whiskey bottle from the table.

He scratched his head and let out a loud belch. The room teetered a bit to the left, and he struggled to regain his equilibrium. He felt like he'd just stepped out of the saddle of an owlhead horse. Peering around the Durham-clouded saloon, he concentrated on focusing on his surroundings. The red-flowered wallpaper shimmied and a painting of an overly endowed nude did a two-step on the wall. Low-turned wall lanterns threw anemic light and clumpy sawdust lay across the floor.

On a stage that jutted into the bar-room proper, a willowy redhead in a blue sateen bodice warbled 'You Naughty, Naughty Men' in a voice as pleasant as a lovesick coyote howling. A few soiled doves were straightening out chairs, collecting glasses, unwatched greenbacks and silver dollars.

Near the back, he noticed the Apache whore named Smells Like Buffalo guarding a door that led to a back

The Deadly Doves

area. She was big as a galldamn bunkhouse and the ugliest Injun he'd ever laid eyes on.

Whip reckoned it was a bit past 1 a.m and most of the cowboys had staggered out of the Rusty Spur – one of Carajo, New Mexico's three saloons – about an hour ago because they had to rise with false dawn and tend to the local ranches' workings.

Two doves cast Whip a 'look' and he managed a lopsided grin. His chest puffed out and he swaggered, staggered, stumbled over to the polished bar and deposited himself on a stool, banging down the whiskey bottle.

Whip considered himself quite a ladies' man, even with his uncomplimentary horseflesh-and-dung cologne. Fact, that's half the reason he had stayed late: he reckoned after a night of sidling up to the cowhands that wandered into the Rusty Spur, any of the doves would be all-fired pleased to have him ride drag. After they drained them cowboys dry they needed a warm body to bed down with, and hell and tarnation he'd be late at the Double H if that were the case.

Whip hoisted the bottle to his lips and gulped the remaining whiskey. Slamming it down, he stared at the empty bottle. Damn sorry sight. He thumped his fist on the bar and blew out a disgusted grunt. 'Hey, Fala, h'bout 'nother whishkey?'

Fala, an auburn-haired woman of about forty built along the lines of a whey-bellied mule, yanked a bottle from the hutch, grabbed a glass and filled it, then slid it in front of Whip. She watched as he slurped at the brownish liquid, coppery eyes intent.

Whip glanced up, gave her a grin. She was lumpy and bulging in too galldamn many of the wrong places – a cinched corset and red sateen bodice accentuated these fleshy abundances – and wore more than what could be considered a generous amount of kohl and kewpie-doll pancake, but she'd do if he were pressed. Fact, since his Hopi squaw had ridden off with the town preacher and most of Whip's meager possessions, most anything in petticoats would pay the bill right nicely.

Fala gave him a peculiar look, one that penetrated even his less than temperate state. He fought the urge to shiver as it suddenly dawned on him where he'd seen that look before: in the eyes of a mountain cat right before it pounced on a deer.

Whip swallowed, suddenly feeling like a wobbly fawn.

As if she had drawn a blind across her eyes, the look vanished and she gave him what he took for a smile, but wouldn't have bet on it as a sure thing. Least not with the cards he'd been drawing lately.

'Late night for a weekday, ain't it, gent?' Fala's voice carried a husky quality that brought the mountain lion image back to his whiskey-soaked mind.

'Yeah. Takin' tomorrow off work at the Double H. Luck's been right bad lately. Had to take me a day job breaking them wild horses Lockwood Hawkins got hisself to replace the ones that got stoled. Plumb sick of the place. Reckon I need a little time to myself.'

Fala nodded, her double chin nodding a beat behind. 'Well, you jest take good care of yourself, honey pie. You're one of our most valued customers. I'd sure hate to see anything happen to you.'

'Happen to me?' His brow furrowed.

'Sure thing, honeybun. Might say I've taken a personal likin' to you.'

Whip's face brightened and a lushy smile glazed his wet lips. Well, now he was gettin' somewhere. Fala might have been the last on his list for night companions, but he wasn't in the frame of mind or luck to be choosy. He glanced into Fala's coppery eyes and she grinned and he got that lion-food feeling again. 'Don't say?' he got out at last, unable to think of anything better.

Fala nodded. With a slight wave of her arm, the flab where her triceps should have been dancing, she beckoned over two doves, who slid on to stools beside Whip. The cloying, sickly – not to mention copious – odor of perfume assailed his nostrils, mixing with sour whiskey on the redhead's breath and the stench of stale cigarettes on the other's. Both girls' eyes were glazed with a vacant, disinterested look, but Whip suddenly felt like a peacock.

Did lions eat peacocks?

Fala smiled her lioness smile. 'Would you like Ambrosia and Wailai to see you upstairs, sugar?'

Judas H. Priest, jackpot! He looked at Ambrosia, whose coral-daubed face held absolutely no expression that he could see, then at Wailai, searching deep into her dark 'breed eyes for some sign of something – lust, need, even disgust, but he saw nothing.

'Hell, yes! Reckon I'm as randy as a three-balled bull!' Ambrosia's hands slid up to Whip's face and she pulled him close, kissing his lips wetly, the taste of whiskey on her breath almost as strong as what was in his glass. Behind him, Wailai slipped a packet filled with white powder from the valley of her purple bodice-heaved bosoms and dumped the contents into his whiskey. The liquor foamed, subsiding quickly as the powder dissolved.

Whip drew back from Ambrosia and turned to Wailai, hoping to get her to second Ambrosia's lushy kiss. Wailai, lion-cub smile in place, pressed her hands to his chest and held him back.

'Later,' she whispered.

Whip wiped drool from the corner of his mouth. 'Awright.' He didn't have a whole lot of coherency to debate her with.

Behind him the last of the customers shuffled through the batwings and the doors creaked as they swung. Whip barely noticed.

'Drink up, sugar pie.' Fala leaned over the bar and he forced his gaze from her generous top. He hauled the glass to his lips, gulping down the whiskey in expectation of what was going to be the night to end all nights for Whip Foley.

Wait . . .

Something was wrong. Things looked . . . *different*. The room took on a sepia color. The heat from the potbellied stove in back felt suddenly overpowering, despite the cool autumn breeze flowing through the batwings. He blinked.

'Judas H. Priest—' He clamped his mouth shut as everything swept dangerously sideways. He had the inclination to pitch off his stool with it. The not-so-gentle hands of Wailai thrust him back into a straightened position.

The surroundings settled for a moment. 'Wh-what happened?' Whip mumbled.

'Why whatever do you mean, sugar?' That lioness look – hungry, eager – sprang on to Fala's face again.

'The room, it, it – galldamn!' Whip's world lurched sideways, or, more accurately, diagonally. He pitched forward. The last thing he recollected was the sawdust-covered floor careening towards him.

A dull, throbbing murmur of voices penetrated Whip's mind, which was wrapped in a cocoon of semi-blackness. He had been – where? At the saloon; that was it.

At the saloon, with two doves and Fala. Then nothing.

Whip struggled to swim up through the black sea, pulling himself on to a flicker of driftwood light. He stared up at the ceiling. Jittering weak light danced from the chandelier like glowing goblins. He focused on something, a weird symbol, whose meaning he didn't know, painted on to the ceiling.

The Rusty Spur! Tarnation, he must still be at the Rusty Spur. He recollected that symbol – a three-barred F – being on the ceiling and floor, though he had never bothered to ask why or what it meant and rightly never gave a lick.

Whip took the next step on the trail to consciousness. At least he tried to. He struggled to sit up, found himself unable to do so. Waiting a moment, he tried to right himself again, failed. This time he realized what held him: ropes. He was lashed to a table like a roped bull. He was also, he discovered as a cool breeze wafted over him, nekked as the day he was birthed.

Dull panic crept into Whip's mind and his heart stuttered. He wasn't sure at first what boogered him, but even with half his spurs jangling he knew something was wrong. Puredee bad wrong.

'What's the matter, honey pie? Can't hold your whiskey?' The husky voice cut through the dirge-like chanting – that's what the murmur of voices was, he realized now, some sort of Indian chanting – and slapped him totally awake.

A husky laugh followed and he twisted his head sideways to see Fala, dressed in some sort of black ceremonial robe. Horizontal black and white streaks adorned her face, kohl darkened her eyes. Buffalo teeth hung from a sinew cord at her neck; they clacked like skeletons kissing against the weird pendant she wore – a replica of the strange symbol on the ceiling and floor.

He cranked his head the opposite way, saw more robed figures standing in a loose circle – the doves, Ambrosia, Wailai, as well as a few regulars. They gazed at him with grim expectant glares.

'Wh-what are you doin' to me?' His voice jittered, but held no trace of a slur.

Fala ignored him. She extracted a Bowie knife from her robe; the blade caught the flickering candlelight – the candles rested on various tables throughout the room – and flashed frozen diamonds across his body.

'N-n-n-nooo!' Whip stammered, shaking his head. His mouth made fish movements and his vocal cords froze momentarily in fright. The dull panic of a moment ago became white hot terror.

Fala laughed, a sound from the deepest cave. 'Let the ceremony begin!'

'Hail in the name of Inkatani, the all-wise one,' the girls droned. One of them began to beat a buffalo-hide drum.

'Oh, great owlman who walks all over the night, rain your blessings upon us!' Fala's husky voice climbed in pitch. Her face twisted. 'I beseech you, Inkatani! Accept our sacrifice. Let it carry our message strong and clear to the one called Hawkins. Let him cower in fear and return what he has taken from us. Let us fulfill our destiny! The day of the Apache warrior is at hand!'

Whip shrieked.

The doves ignored him, continuing their chanting. 'Hail in the name of Inkatani, he who walks all over the night. . . .'

'Bring it!' Fala gestured sharply with an arm. Wailai stepped from the circle and went to the pot-bellied stove near the back. Whip tried to see what she was doing but she had her back to him. Slowly turning, she came towards him and Whip struggled furiously against his bonds. His heart slammed into his ribs and his eyes widened in horror.

Wailai stepped up to the table, clutching a glowing branding iron in her dark hands. She poised it above Whip, waiting.

'Begin!' Fala's eyes glittered, vicious.

Wailai started the iron downward, towards Whip's belly. A sizzling filled the air. The acrid stench of burning flesh assailed his nostrils. He screeched as pain burned into him like hellfire.

Wailai pulled the iron away and when Whip looked down he saw the strange three-barred F seared into his flesh, its edges livid. He shrieked again.

A crash sounded from the back of the saloon and Wailai jolted, jerking the iron up. A giggle flowed.

Fala's head snapped around and the doves looked towards a door at the rear leading to a short hall and back room. Another crash, as if someone had walked into a wall.

'Who is it?' screamed Fala, anger twisting her face.

The door flew open. A girl in a peek-a-boo blouse staggered out, giggling, clutching at the door frame to keep her balance.

Fala's eyes narrowed. 'Who is that?'

'One of the new girls,' Wailai answered, contempt in her voice. 'She must have passed out in the back. She is pretty heavy on the laudanum. She is not initiated.'

'She's seen too much, then.' Fala nudged her head towards the dove clinging to the door and three girls stepped from the circle. Going to her, they grabbed her arms and hurled her towards Fala. She stopped giggling and fear invaded her laudanum-clouded eyes.

'You have soiled our ritual.' An insane light glittered in Fala's eyes. She let out a shriek of unbridled anger.

She spun, thrust the Bowie knife above her head and plunged it into Whip's chest. Whip saw it coming, felt fear surge through his veins like poison, felt the searing heat of the blade that now protruded from his ribs. Then blackness invaded his mind, this time for ever.

'Take her!' Fala commanded, with a violent nudge of her head, indicating the dove. 'We'll use her to complete the ceremony tomorrow night since she blundered into it.'

'Why don't we just initiate her?' asked Wailai. 'We can always use more followers.'

'Now? After what she's witnessed? I don't think that's possible. No, better not to jeopardize our plans. One less whore doesn't matter.' Fala hesitated then added, 'And make sure Hawkins gets this.' She nodded to Whip's body. 'It makes me sick just looking at him.' Fala turned and grabbed a handful of Whip's stringy hair. With her other hand she plucked the Bowie knife from his chest and ruby and diamond flashed from the blade as she began to saw into his scalp.

After, she dismissed the doves and they drifted up the stairs to their rooms. Wailai went to the table and hastily untied and dressed Whip's body, then wrapped it in a buffalo-hide blanket.

A few moments later, four of the doves returned along with Ambrosia, who was dressed in a dark blouse and trousers, hair pulled back and kohl smudged across her features so she would blend with the darkness. Wailai directed the doves in the disposal of Whip's lifeless form. They carried him out the back way to a waiting buckboard, where they unceremoniously dumped him in the back. Wailai and Ambrosia climbed into the driver's seat and the half-breed Apache clucked her tongue. The buckboard rattled along the back road then out on to a hardpacked trail. An owl whooed and night creatures sang and slithered in the darkness of the chilled autumn night. A coyote moaned a mournful howl.

'Here!' hissed Wailai, drawing the buckboard to a stop. In the distance she could see the dull lights from the main house of the Hawkins Double H ranch compound.

They rolled Whip's body on to the ground, standing over it a moment like buzzards.

'Isn't this a little obvious?' asked Ambrosia.

'So?' replied Wailai. 'Nobody will miss him and nobody will care. But Hawkins will know. That's all that matters.'

Ambrosia laughed, a sound as frigid as the night.

'Let us go,' said Wailai. 'We have other matters to attend to.'

The girls climbed into the driver's seat and Wailai sent the buckboard towards town, blackness swallowing them, leaving the body of Whip Foley behind to the coyotes.

TWO

Marshal Zachary Taylor Revere yawned and dumped a can of beans into the wooden bowl couched in the crook of his arm. Dressed in a red union suit, he shuffled across the kitchen, stepping over Oliver, the chubby tabby cat who lay sprawled on the floor. Oliver cocked an eye open, giving him a put-out look, then went back to whatever it was cats thought about. Zach reckoned it was probably trout or some such. He poised at the hallway entrance.

'Come on, Billy, get outta the saddle!' he shouted to his son, who had been known to squeeze a few more minutes of shuteye than he should, as eight-year-old boys were wont to do. 'You'll be late for school again. That new school marm'll tan your hide but good.'

'Comin', Pa!' returned an exasperated yell from down the hall.

'Godamighty, you're as stubborn as a mule and twice as slow!' Zach teased back, managing a sleepy grin.

'Tarnation, I am!' he heard his son grumble back.

'Don't cuss, boy!' Zach tried to make it sound as gruff as possible.

Puncheon floor cool beneath his feet, he shuffled over to the counter and set down the bowl. Plunking a heavy skillet on a burner of the cast-iron stove, he set half a dozen pieces of bacon to frying and transferred the beans to an iron pan, heating them up.

As the smoky scent of sizzling pork filled the air, Zach sighed, prolonging the expression. *Routine* Godamighty he was getting plumb sick of it. How long had he been doing this, hauling his carcass out of the big down bed an hour early every morning to cook Billy and himself breakfast, getting his son off to school and himself off to work at the Carajo marshal's office to be badgered by a less-than-understanding mayor for being a few minutes late?

Too long.

And he reckoned everyday it galled him all the more. Blame it all, didn't that mayor have anything better to do anyhow? Hell and tarnation, when Potter hired him to keep law in the cowtown he'd neglected to tell he'd be regulated to mundane tasks like breaking up the occasional scuffle at one of the saloons and hauling in some drunk cowhand for pissing on the boardwalk. To a retired manhunter it felt like purgatory and holy hell all rolled into one.

Hell, it didn't even pay that much and he and Laura had quickly found this small ranch beyond their means. That's why she had taken that job at the Hawkins place, sewing them fancy dresses for haughty cattle- and horse-rancher's wives and learning Hawkins's four-year-old daughter after the man's wife died giving birth to her. She made damn near double his pay and blamed if he couldn't help feeling irked about it and for reasons he couldn't quite get a bridle on, he felt frustration building, cinching his innards, restlessness. He knew it wouldn't be long before something went pop; he saw the signs: lack of concentration at work, a lassitude at home, and an eye that had done all too much roving lately. How long before he gave in?

How long before he said chuck it all and surrendered to the feeling, the impulse, to another woman?

Godamighty! What was he talking about? He loved Laura. Didn't he? He had the idyllic life: a beautiful wife, a healthy son, a good job, the ranch and a hell of a lot less risk of seeing the underside of a boneyard than when he hired out his gun for a living. What did he have to complain about?

A noise in back of him broke his reverie and he turned to see Laura coming into the kitchen. Her blonde hair was piled high atop her head, face framed by tiny curls. A simple blue dress with leg-of-mutton sleeves hugged her old-fashioned curves and a straw hat, tied with a ribbon under the chin, sat atop her head.

'Top of the mornin',' he said, trying to show some enthusiasm. 'The coach isn't here yet.'

'Zach, please, don't be like that. You know it's the only way and Mr Hawkins is right kind sendin' a man for me. He even promised to let me borrow the buckboard when I pick up Billy later this week.'

'I've heard Hawkins described many a way but kind sure as spit ain't one of 'em.'

Laura frowned, an expression he'd seen far too much of lately. 'He's not that bad.'

Zach raised an eyebrow. 'Ain't he? He's damn near bought Carajo and I reckon I still don't cotton to you workin' for him.'

She blew out a exasperated sigh and her lips took that peculiar little stubborn turn he didn't like. 'Don't see much choice, Zach. We need the money.'

'Not from him.' Stubbornness was something Laura didn't have a monopoly on, he reckoned.

'Zach, we've been over this a hundred times. It's not just Hawkins and his money. It's something between us. You got some kind of ghost chasin' you and until you decide to turn around and face it things won't get better.'

Zach grunted, irritation prickling him. Hell, it *was* Hawkins and his money, at least a goodly part of it. Wasn't it? The scalawag damn near owned Carajo and pulled the mayor's strings to boot. What it boiled down to was Hawkins was vying to set himself up as cattle king of the area and anybody with any sense of future in Carajo worked for him, especially the mayor. For all intents and purposes the mayor worked for Hawkins and Zach Revere worked for the mayor. Which essentially meant Hawkins employed both members of the Revere family.

Godamighty. It was a hell of a thing, having your strings pulled. He reckoned it might have been that way when he hired out his gun for various cattlemen associations, but at least then he had the right to refuse the jobs.

Things had changed since he met Laura and settled down, since Billy had come along. Maybe he hadn't been quite ready for pasture, though, hell, he knew his reflexes had slowed enough to get him killed the moment some faster gun took a notion to test his sand. Despite that he yearned for what he was.

Maybe Laura was right. Maybe that ghost was chasin' him.

The notion prickled him, and his eyes hardened. 'Godamighty, Laura, seems like I never get to see you 'cept in passin'. Man's got needs, you know. I didn't get hitched to have myself just some saloon gal who came and went as pretty as you please.'

'Zach, it isn't that way and you know it! Once we get the ranch paid off things will be different. We've got a few things to work out, but a lot of marriages do.'

'A lot of marriages don't have a wife workin' for a man who owns the pot you piss in! Most women in the West stay home and are waitin' on their man at the end of a day. Hell, we don't need to work things out, we just need to spend time together, doin' things the way we used to in the beginnin'.'

'You know we've had to make some adjustments since Billy came along. We didn't need this job then.'

'Reckon I know that. We've been over it and over it. Hell, you know I don't like to talk about things like that. Ain't the way I was raised.'

She put a hand on his shoulder, face growing softer. He saw compassion bloom like soft pink roses in her eyes and a glow of emotion that had once made him love her like no other woman. 'You never like to talk about your feelings; that's a lot of the problem. You keep your notions all inside till they turn into powerful yearnin's you can't abide with.'

His shoulders dropped and he sighed. 'Yeah, reckon you're right, it's my fault. I'll try to keep my man ways to myself.'

'Don't indulge me, Zach. You know I hate it when you do it and I don't rightly deserve it.' Her face turned harder.

'Sorry.' Eyes narrowing, a defeated look wandered across his face. His head turned towards the window as the sound of a buckboard and horse hooves drawing closer reached his ears.

'Your ride's here,' he said with no emotion, though something in his belly tightened.

She rose on her toes and kissed his cheek, face remaining serious. 'We'll talk tonight – promise me?'

'I may be late again. I reckon the mayor might have another drunk falling off his horse for me to haul to the hoosegow.'

The Dead

She gave him an exasper[ated look] up.' A hint of a grin turned word for you with Mayor Po[tter] his sister's princess gown to[o]

'Now who's indulging?'

'Mayor Potter has faith i[n you] wouldn't have hired you if [he didn't think you could] keep the law in Carajo. You j[ust need to show some] understanding.' Laura uttered a mischievous chuckle.

Zach sighed, the feeling of defeat strengthening. 'Even the gods didn't tie Hercules' hands after tellin' him to clean the stables.'

'Mr Hawkins is waitin' on me, I have to go.' Laura kissed his cheek again then hurried out.

Zach collapsed against the counter, frustration eating at him as he heard the rattle of the buckboard and the clop-clopping of hooves recede into the distance.

Tarnation, you're a stubborn sonofabitch, he chided himself. She's tryin' the best she can. Are you more jealous of her working for Hawkins or because she's contented to be aiming towards something in this union while you're pinin' over days gone by?

Zach heaved a heavy sigh and turned to see Billy, a brown-haired boy with an impish twist to his mouth and slightly bucked teeth, sliding into a seat at the heavy plank table. He was dressed in a blue-checked cotton shirt, trousers and suspenders.

'Whatta *you* want, boy?' Zach asked half-heartedly, trying to grin.

'Breakfast,' answered Billy. 'Two eggs, bacon, toast, orange juice and some of Ma's biscuits.'

'You're gettin' beans and bacon and you'll like 'em.'

'How 'bout the biscuits?' prodded Billy.

Zach felt like saying his ma hadn't been home long

...ther making any, but reined his tongue. ...the ones hidden in the cupboard were for

...esh out,' he muttered, going to the stove to finish ...oking the bacon. The beans were over-heated dry and lumpy, stuck to the pan. He scraped them into a tin plate and served up Billy, then slumped into a chair at the table, opting for cold Arbuckle's himself.

'You ain't eatin' your own cooking again, Pa.' A sly look crossed Billy's eyes as he pushed at the lumpy beans with his fork.

'How old did you say you were, boy?' Zach cocked an eyebrow.

'Old enough to know over-cooked beans.' The boy smirked.

'Reckon you said you wanted your chores added to?' Zach reached across the table and grabbed yesterday's edition of the Carajo *Tribune*, which he had not gotten a chance to read. It would likely be more of the same, telling how Hawkins owned this or that, what Hawkins would do once the railroad came through, how much good Hawkins was accomplishing for the town.

Galldamn Hawkins and his Double H spread right to hell and back, anyway.

'I got half a dozen chores now!' Billy complained with a touch of sarcasm Zach knew the boy had inherited from him.

'That few, huh? Reckon I'm too easy on ya!'

'Tarnation, you ain't!' Billy gave a disgusted snort and with a grimace forced down a forkful of beans.

'Don't cuss – and don't say "ain't".' Zach winked. 'Your ma'll take hard soap to your mouth, you keep it up.'

'We gotta get ridin', Pa.' Billy gulped the rest of his

The Deadly Doves

beans in four huge mouthfuls, then pushed himself out of his chair and deposited his dish on the counter. He reached up and opened a cabinet, pulling a small checkered cloth-covered basket from the shelf and sneaking out a wildberry biscuit that his mother had secretly stashed there for supper. He squirreled it away in his pocket, set the basket back on the shelf and closed the cabinet.

Zach folded his paper and stood. 'Go get Gertrude saddled up. I'll be right on out.'

'Aw, Pa – that glue again?' Billy shook his head in disgust.

'Gerty's a blamed fine piece of horseflesh, boy, and don't you forget it!' Zach responded with mock anger.

Resignation crossed Billy's face, as well as a hint of embarrassment at having his father ride him to school on the 'Glue', as his son was wont to call her. He scooped up his schoolbooks from the counter and went through the pantryway to the door. Zach heard it bang shut as he gulped the remainder of his coffee and tossed his paper on the counter. Ambling down the hall to his bedroom, he dressed and strapped on his gunbelt, sliding the Colt Peacemaker in and out of its holster three times, a habit from his manhunter days, where the slightest snag could get a body buried. Going back to the kitchen, he pulled on his buffalo-hide coat, grabbed his Stetson and followed Billy out to the stable.

Gerty was a whey-bellied old bay who moved slightly faster than a turtle hoping not to be soup. The old girl was saddled and snorting in the early morning sunlight and nickered as he stepped into the saddle. Reaching down, he scooped Billy up and into the saddle behind him. He turned to the boy with a grin. 'Where to, pard?'

'Tarnation, Pa, don't make this worse than it already is.' Billy slumped in the saddle, attempting to hide himself from the watchful eyes of any of his friends who might be walking to the schoolhouse along the way. Zach chuckled as he gigged the horse into a lazy gait. Gerty had one speed and that was it.

The shroud of canyon maple, cottonwood and lodgepole pine hugging either side of the trail gave way to the dirt- and dung-coated streets of Carajo. Its horseshoe arrangement of false-fronted and adobe buildings glimmered in the brilliant autumn sunlight. Diamonds of light glinted from troughs and windows. Early risers shuffled along the boardwalk towards the Dusty Shamrock eatery.

Guiding the bay down Carajo's main street, he purposely waved at the kids he knew to be Billy's friends while pointing to the back of him to make certain they saw Billy was aboard. Meanwhile, Billy tried to shrink further into the saddle, face reddening.

After dropping Billy off at school, Zach headed towards the marshal's office. He felt the gentle swaying of Gerty beneath him and sighed. 'Hell, old girl, you an' me make quite a pair. Reckon both of us ain't good for much sometimes but we keep on tryin' all the same.'

The horse snorted and seemed little interested in its station and Zach reckoned the beast was the luckier of the two. He recollected the days he had ridden her across the boundless plains, the wind at his back and the scent of fresh spring wildflowers in his nostrils. Freedom and worth, bought and paid for at the barrel of a Peacemaker and despite the way some folks looked at manhunting he always felt a certain sense of duty and pride at bringing down hardcases and cattle thieves. He reckoned there was at least a little honor in doing what a body thought was right.

The Deadly Doves

Now? Now he had a god-awful restlessness inside and the scent of decaying autumn leaves in his nostrils. A season of dying and a feeling of aching loneliness and days gone past.

Zachary Taylor Revere, aged forty-three and feeling every bit of it, slumped in the saddle, feeling sorry for himself and not giving a damn if he did. His dark-brown hair more and more over the past year had started to thin, recede just a hoot and a holler, and go gray at the temples. Lines creased the flesh around his eyes and mouth; he swore those lines hadn't been there just last week. He looked more and more like his pa every day, at least the way his pa had looked at this age.

Clint Revere was dead now, but Zach still felt bothered by the fact that they had never quite gotten along the way a father and son should. Pa had never approved of manhunting, killing for money. He never saw the justice in it, the sense of duty. He only saw damnation at the hands of his avenging righteous God and when Zach left his pa had called him a murderer and thumped his Bible until Zach couldn't stand to hear the burning words in his ears – *'Glory be to those who preserve life and not smite it! Glory be to all except you, Zachary Taylor Revere, may your sorry hide burn in the fires of everlasting Hell!'*

Zach wondered if his pa would approve of marshaling, legal killing in the name of justice and a tin star, but the old man had taken the chance of Zach ever finding out with him to his grave.

Zach drew up and stepped from the saddle, tethering Gerty to the hitch rail outside his office.

Entering, Zach flung his hat on his desk and collapsed into his chair, groaning at the mound of dodgers he wouldn't be getting to because the mayor would be wanting him to chase down some runaway mule or stop a soiled dove from beating the balls off some poor cowboy who'd somehow forgotten he'd spent most of his wages on whiskey and was broke till next month.

At the desk directly across from him Deputy Jesse James Buchanan looked up and made a clucking noise.

'*What*?' Zach leaned his chair back on two legs, letting his coat fall open to reveal the tin star pinned to his chest.

Buchanan, a younger man with dark hair, spectacles and an angular face, shook his head and made a *puft* sound. 'A might testy, ain't we, Zachary?'

'Just come right out with it if you've got somethin' to say, Jess. I've important matters to 'tend to, such as old ladies fallin' off mules.'

'Fifteen minutes, Zachary. The mayor will probably dance a jig for you bein' only a little late this time.'

'I reckon. Maybe he won't notice.'

Buchanan's laugh sounded like a mule braying. 'He *always* notices. He sits in his little hidy-hole over his office after he slips one of them Spur doves out his room 'fore dawn and watches jest to see what time you sashay in here.'

Zach grunted. 'Tarnation, but I live for the day I slip one by him.'

'You don't have that many years left.'

'You ain't joshin',' said Zach, though a smile forced its way on to his lips. He leaned forward and pulled a worn folder from the mess on his desk – his most recent case. Routine. Always routine. He did the same thing every morning.

At least this one was wrapped up: the Conroy woman, ninety-three and taking the notion she was spry beyond her years, had got bucked from her old mule and ended up being hauled in a wagon to the undertakers.

The door burst open, snapping Zach's reverie. He looked up to see the none-too-pleased face of Mayor Potter, a dark-haired man with a Mex look if not name. The door was just big enough to accommodate him and Zach reckoned if His Honor kept puttin' away ten meals a day at Millie's place it wouldn't be much longer. The mayor made a blustery sound that shuddered cheeks plumped as jowly as Mrs Deekins' prize hog.

'You are fifteen minutes late, Zachary Taylor Revere. I ought to fire you.' Mayor Potter put his hands on his hips and eyed Zach with serious reprimand. Zach almost laughed. He wondered how such a barrel of a man could look so prissy sometimes.

'Hell, don't give me special treatment – it looks bad in front of the deputy.' Zach grinned, knowing he was pushing his luck.

Across from him. Buchanan stifled a laugh.

'What are *you* snickering at?' snapped the mayor, pinning Buchanan with his gaze. The deputy shrugged and went back to a stack of wanted posters held been looking through.

'You jest come here to tell me I'm late again or this a social call?' Zach hoped it sounded as sarcastic as he meant it to.

Mayor Potter bristled; something about it reminded Zach of an old fat chicken. 'Have you finished with that Conroy case yet?'

'Just wrapped it up. Simple case of being muleheaded.'

'That isn't funny, Zachary Taylor Revere.' The big mayor's small eyes glittered with just about every expression except amusement, emphasizing his proclamation.

'So you came to tell me you don't like my humor?'

The mayor harrumphed. Zach had never really heard anyone harrumph before and by damn, he hadn't missed anything.

'Whip Foley was murdered last night. You know the type he was and it is not surprising. But he was deposited on the Double H ranch and Mr Hawkins is far from pleased about it.'

'I bet he ain't.' Zach ran a finger over his upper lip, the news was surprising, despite Whip Foley's reputation as a no-good.

'He had no money on him and you simply must take yourself over there and clean this up right way. We can't have such things happening in Carajo. It isn't civilized.'

'We can't have Hawkins inconvenienced, you mean.' Zach didn't bother to cover his contempt.

'Need I remind you who pays your lovely wife's salary, Zachary?' The mayor gave him a smug look that made Zach want to kick him in the teeth.

'Reckon I remind myself of it all too frequently, Mayor.'

'You simply madden me sometimes, Zachary.' The barrel-built man frowned and shook his head with the grace of a society lady. 'Honestly!'

Zach grunted. 'Sometimes? I must not be workin' hard enough at it.'

'Take yourself out to the Double H right this moment. You are the marshal here and I expect you to behave as such.' The man's beady eyes pinned Zach and he frowned.

'Yes, sir, your honor.'

Mayor Potter grumbled and turned, stalking out the door, across the boardwalk and towards the Dusty Shamrock.

The Deadly Doves

Buchanan glanced up, a smirk on his face, eyebrow cocked. 'Don't you ever worry you'll push him too far? He may just fire you one of these days.'

'Pshaw! I reckon he cottons to the aggravation. Some of them prissy gents are like that, I swan.'

'I dunno, I think you underestimate him, or at least underworry about him.'

'You reckon? Hell, I figure what it boils down to is that I really don't give a diddly damn if he does fire me.'

'I know you're a might worn out, Zachary, but I think you truly like it here. Why else would you stay and tolerate the likes of him?'

'What else us old glues got to do?'

'Maybe you need a vacation.'

'Tarnation, not now.' Zach pushed back his chair and rose. 'Mr Foley is waitin' on me. Wouldn't want to let him down.'

THREE

A chill made the air brisk and brittle and the sun, blazing from the frosty-blue autumn sky, honey-coated the multicolored leaves and evergreen boughs.

Zach slowed Gerty as he approached the Double H ranch compound, a heaviness in his soul that the coldness didn't help. The scent of decaying leaves perfumed the air and reminded him of death and dying and lives snapped short by his own gun. He'd never really given it much thought when he was a manhunter; the only good hardcase was a dead one, he reckoned, though there was always that specter of emptiness, of life wasted. As the years had worn on it had become stronger, and he had grown more remorseful.

Hell, a manhunter shouldn't feel remorse, should he?

A human being should. . . .

He uttered a low laugh, a shiver working its way up his back as he drew up in front of the five men standing around a form wrapped in a buffalo-hide blanket. Stepping from the saddle, he walked towards the men.

Three of them appeared to be ranch hands. One of them, a fellow who looked like a Mex, flicked his smoke at the form and laughed, the other two hands joining in.

The fourth, older man he recognized – and not without a twisting in his belly – as Lockwood Hawkins the ranch owner. The man had a hard expression on his stubbly face and something else in his cold blue eyes that took Zach a moment to pinpoint. Fear. Vague, undefined, but there none the less. Zach wondered why.

The last man was dressed in a cheap suit with a gold watch-chain dangling from his vest pocket and a notepad in his hand. He was scribbling something with the stub of a pencil and Zach eyed him curiously.

Stopping, he glanced at the body, then at Hawkins, holding the rancher's cold gaze for a moment. Zach had encountered his type often as a manhunter, a pompous controlling sonofabitch used to ordering hands and hired guns alike. The sun set by their clocks and rose when they said let there be light and Zach was inclined to tell them right up front he did things his way or no way. But that was the old days and Hawkins damn near had him beholden now.

'Marshal.' Hawkins gave a slight nod and a condescension hung in his voice, as if he were talking to one of his hired hands.

Zach nudged his head towards the body. 'What happened?'

The ranch owner shrugged. 'Boys found it here a little past dawn. Foley was workin' for me, breakin' wild horses to replace the ones I've lost. Waste of skin if you ask me, but a damn fine horse buster.'

Zach nodded. He had known horses and cattle had been disappearing from the Double H compound for a spell, though whoever was doing it was sure as hell practiced and sneaky as a priest in a cathouse. Some suspected Apache were responsible, though they had been sent to reservations two years back and it seemed unlikely to Zach. Still he had never found evidence to the contrary, nor evidence at all for that matter.

'Inclined to agree, Hawkins, though a man deserves better'n to be dumped alone on the ground, I reckon, even a man like Whip Foley.'

Hawkins raised a condescending eye brow. 'You reckon? I don't, Marshal. He'd have come back on time and tended to his job he might be kickin' now.'

Zach met the man's cold stare. 'Still a human being, Hawkins, and that gives him a right to die with a little dignity.'

Hawkins gave a derisive laugh that carried a hint of nervousness. 'Don't rightly seem the way a former manhunter would think. Would have bet you killed plenty of horse thieves without much thought as to their dignity.'

Zach felt his belly cinch. 'Always made sure they got buried. Never left even the most vicious hardcase to the buzzards.'

'Just get him off my land, Marshal. I don't give a donkey's ass if you send him to Hades with honors, just don't do it here.'

Zach took a deep breath, feeling his animosity for the rancher grow. Godamighty, he hated the thought of Laura working for this man.

Zach knelt, forearms on his knees, and peered at the body wrapped in the hide blanket. Strange. He wondered why someone would bother wrapping Whip and dumping him here, and he wondered if it had anything to do with the recent thievery at the compound.

'You say his pockets were empty?' Zach saw that as the only motive. He could see Whip going to a saloon and meeting up with a hardcase passing through or the like and winding up empty of greenbacks, though it didn't explain this completely. He looked up at Hawkins.

The rancher glanced at the suited man scribbling on his pad and Zach's attention shifted to see the man look up as gazes fell upon him.

'Why, I said that, Marshal Revere, surely I did.'

'Who the hell are you?' Zach cocked an eyebrow.

'Name's Bateman, yessir, Bateman. Work for the Carajo *Tribune* and I'm writin' the next best-selling dime novel 'bout the recent thievery here at the Double H. Going to make Mr Hawkins famous, yessir, famous.'

Zach groaned. Just what he needed, some purple-prose word-jockey making things worse. 'How the hell, you find out about this?

Bateman was a lanky man in his late thirties and his suit hung on him like a frock coat on a scarecrow. The reporter got an indignant set to his sharp chin and a lazy left eye wandered disconcertingly. He had ears like a mule's.

'Why, I saw our fine mayor on his way to your office this morning and noticed he was a little excited about something, yessir, excited. I stopped him and he was only too glad to give me the story.'

'I'll jest reckon he was.' A note of disgust hung in Zach's voice.

'Why, yessir, he was, he was, indeed. I rode right out here to find Mr Hawkins and his men and explained his predicament would make a fine book for my readers.'

Zach wasn't in the mood to be tactful. 'You don't write fine books, Mr Bateman; you write cow flop.'

One of the hands laughed and Bateman's face turned crimson. Breath steamed out his nostrils and he looked like a skinny bull who'd just found his horns stuck in the side of the barn and couldn't pull them out.

'Well, call it what you want, Marshal Revere, but I assure you my readers would not agree.'

Zach eyed him. 'How you know my name, Bateman?'

'I know everything in Carajo; it's my job as chief scribe.'

'Yeah?' A devilish light played in Zach's eyes. 'Who stole Mr Hawkins's horses and cattle then?'

Bateman's face turned redder and more steam seemed to blow out his nose. He went silent, obviously fuming and Hawkins uttered a chopped laugh.

'You checked for greenbacks?' A slight note of accusation laced Zach's tone as his gaze drilled the reporter.

'Why, yes, it seemed the thing to do, Marshal. Details, you know, yessir, details.'

'Reckon Whip didn't need 'em where he was goin',' muttered Zach, nodding.

'That ain't the half of it,' the hand who had disrespectfully flung the cigarette at the corpse put in and Zach peered at him.

'Who're you?'

'Mr Hawkins's *segundo*, Luis Fuego.'

'Whatta you mean that ain't the half of it?'

The second glanced at Hawkins then the other men and all of them suddenly had nervous rabbits scurrying in their eyes.

'Take yourself a looksee, if you've a mind to, Marshal,' said Hawkins, tone grim. 'But make it quick. I got a ranch to run.'

'I'll keep that in mind.' Zach tugged the blanket back and a gasp escaped his lips. 'Cristamighty!' Glancing up at Hawkins, he saw the fear in the rancher's eyes grow stronger. One of the hands turned away and only Bateman seemed unmoved by the sight.

Zach forced himself to look back to the body. 'This man's been scalped . . .' he muttered, eyeing the gory patch of sawed flesh atop Foley's head. In one place naked white bone showed through. A bloody splotch soiled the man's shirt and Zach pulled it open to see a knife wound. Something about it struck Zach's trained inner sense as wrong, but he couldn't pinpoint what it was at the moment.

Zach pulled the hide blanket off completely and looked at Whip's feet, noting the man wore no boots. A puzzled expression turned his features. Then it dawned on him concomitantly what had bothered him about the knife wound area on Whip's chest. He cranked his head around and looked up at Bateman, who was staring at him.

'You notice the guy isn't wearing any boots?' asked Zach.

Bateman shrugged, looked indifferent. 'Reckon I did indeed. Likely they were fancy ones and he lost 'em in a game.'

Zach raised an eyebrow. 'You reckon the man bet his boots? Weather's been right cool lately; you'd think he'd know better.'

Hawkins grunted. 'The fellow was a down-on-his-luck gambler, Marshal. Always right liquored up, too, so he coulda forgot 'em.' Hawkins didn't look like he believed what he was saying.

Zach frowned, knowing it was useless to pursue it. 'That don't explain the knife wound, though.'

Bateman let out a nervous laugh. 'What's to explain, Marshal? Big knife brought down with lots of force. Looks like it went clean through a rib. Probably makes our killer a large male, Apache most like, since the fellow was relieved of his hair.'

'Then why ain't there a slice in his shirt? See' – Zach

jabbed a finger at Whip's chest – 'there's the bloodstain, but the fabric is intact. You think maybe some brave was about to stab him, and Whip said, 'Hey, hold it there, Geronimo, I don't want to ruin my shirt?' Then just as he's gettin' his Injun haircut he decides to button up again?'

Bateman seemed to shrink a little. 'How would I know, Marshal? Maybe the Injun was a lush. Apaches aren't known to hold their firewater, indeed they aren't. Maybe the killer wanted the shirt and got nervous at the last minute and left it.' Bateman's voice held a measure of irritation and Zach felt an equal measure of satisfaction.

'So our killer took the time to put it back on the body?' Zach yanked the blanket back over the body and straightened. 'You're the man with all the answers, Mr Bateman. You tell me why he would take the time to do that instead of just stealin' it.'

Knots formed to either side of Bateman's cheeks. 'I'm sure I don't know, Marshal Revere, indeed I don't. And I do believe no one would care to waste time figuring it out.' Bateman's left eye wandered, righted itself.

'Reckon you're right, Mr Bateman. I jest hope you'll pay a little more attention to your *details* in your dime novel than you are here.'

'I fail to see what details have to do with the town drunk getting killed and savin' us the time wasted on hangin' him eventually anyway.' The reporter got an indignant lilt to his voice.

'You know, Mr Bateman,' said Zach, holding the skinny man's gaze, 'human beings are an odd assortment. Sometimes life takes peculiar twists on them, and they can't handle it so they turn to believin' in snake oil, like our friend Whip, here, maybe.' He glanced at Hawkins, who looked gray and frightened for no reason Zach could fathom. 'Then there are others; reckon they got all they need, maybe even more. They make the right choices but somewhere along the way they lose their sense of compassion.' Zach's gaze drifted back to the reporter. 'Don't lose your compassion, Mr Bateman. Reckon I'd hate to see you without it.'

'What's that supposed to mean, Marshal?' The congenial look disappeared completely from Bateman's face, replaced by open irritation.

'Jest a little friendly advice from a frustrated ex-manhunter, Mr Bateman. Take it or leave it.'

Bateman gave a put-out snort and went back to scribbling notes on his tablet.

Zach gazed at the blanket-covered form again, a niggling little voice inside him telling him there was more to this than some hardcase, out-of-luck gambler ending up on the wrong end of the deal, and he knew that little voice would nag him until he found out what it was.

'Which saloon was he at last night?' Zach peered at Hawkins, who seemed to be getting a hold of himself now.

'How the hell would I know?' Hawkins almost spat.

'The Rusty Spur, most like,' put in one of the hands and Hawkins cast him a corrosive look.

'Obliged. Reckon I'd best check that out.' Zach turned and walked towards Gerty, a cold feeling welling inside unrelated to the weather.

'I want this body off my land, Marshal,' he heard Hawkins yell behind him.

'I'll send the undertaker later today,' Zach shouted back with a slight measure of satisfaction at making Hawkins wait. 'Don't move him in the meantime.'

'Hey—' the rancher started, anger in his voice.

'Is for horses.' Zach laughed and stepped into the saddle.

After contacting the undertaker about seeing to Whip Foley's body, Zach tethered Gerty to the hitch rail and walked along the boardwalk towards the Rusty Spur, one of Carajo's three saloons along with the Golden Parasol and the Silver Saddle. The sight of Whip Foley's scalped remains still made his belly tighten and the more he chewed on it the less he liked it. He saw more to it than a simple killing and he reckoned someone had gone out of their way to make it look like Indians, but he reckoned no Apache would have taken Whip's boots and scalp and redressed him after plunging a knife into his chest. It made no sense.

Unless there was another reason for that corpse being in the condition it was on Hawkins's spread. The rancher had looked frightened, though obviously had tried to hide that fact. Did the murder tie in with the recent hits on the Double H spread? Zach bet it did. Proving it was another matter entirely, however.

Zach reached the saloon entrance and pushed through the batwings, senses immediately assaulted by the reek of stale Durham smoke, sour booze and cheap perfume. His gaze drifted across the room, to the small stage and red flower papering, paintings of overly endowed nude women and clumpy sawdust. His attention lingered a moment on the odd symbol painted on to the floor, a strange three-barred F. Barely showing through the sawdust, it looked like some sort of brand. His gaze traveled upward, to the stairs and landing that led to the rooms and cubicles above, where doves plied their trade of relieving cowhands of their thirty-a-month pay.

The place was deserted at the early hour, save for a

girl, a 'breed, Zach reckoned, sprinkling new sawdust on the floor. He made his way to the polished bar that took up nearly an entire side of the room, and signaled the barkeep, a woman dressed in a red sateen bodice that hoisted her plump bosoms nearly to her chins. Her body was far too lumpy for the outfit, far as he was concerned – and she wore too much coral on her cheeks and kohl around her coppery eyes. From her looks, he reckoned Indian blood ran through her veins. The woman cast him an unreadable look.

'We ain't open for business yet, sugar,' she said.

'I'm not here for pleasure.' Zach drew the side of his coat back to let the tin star show. 'Marshal Zach Revere, ma'am.'

'As in Paul Revere?'

Zach winced inwardly. 'A distant relative, but I'm sure he wouldn't approve of me.'

'What can I do you for, Marshal? This surely ain't a social visit.' The plump 'keep pulled a cloth from beneath the bar and began to wipe off the counter.

'Whip Foley, you know 'im?'

She looked up. 'Reckon I do vaguely. Gent comes in here every so often, spends his pay on whiskey and some of my girls.'

Zach raised an eyebrow. 'Your girls? You own this saloon?'

'Sure as shootin', honey pie. Name's Fala Ellis.'

'Ain't many female saloon owners in these parts.'

'Reckon it's high time there was.'

'Foley come in last night?'

'Might have – why?'

'He's dead. Found him on Double H land this morning.'

'Plumb sorry to hear that.' Zach didn't think she sounded sorry at all. 'Why come here, Marshal? I reckon a gent like Foley had lots of enemies.'

'Reckon it's just a matter of routine, ma'am. Hand from the Double H told me he came here last night. Hoped you might have seen somethin' that might clear up what happened.'

She nodded, but her expression didn't change. 'I see. And what exactly happened to Mr Foley?'

Zach shrugged. He reckoned it didn't matter whether he told her. 'Got himself knifed, and relieved of whatever greenbacks he might have had on him. Got himself an Injun haircut, too.'

'Senseless violence,' said Fala, all too placatingly, Zach thought. 'Downright shame, ain't it?'

'Reckon it is, ma'am – you say he was in here?'

'He stayed 'til closin' time, then left.'

'Alone?'

'I believe he didn't, Marshal. I think he left with Sage.'

'Sage?'

'One of my new gals. Don't know much about her, but seems like she's got herself a hankerin' for losers.'

'Reckon I could have a parley with this Sage?'

Fala shook her head. 'No, as a matter of fact she never came back after leavin' with Whip last night. I sure hope nothin' befell her.'

'Reckon I do too, ma'am.' Zach tried to see behind Fala's stoic expression. She had a look to her he didn't cotton too, a predatory look.

'Anything else I can tell you, Marshal?'

'Reckon not for the moment. Thanks for your time anyway,' Zach pushed himself away from the bar, wondering just what, if anything, he had expected to find here.

'Anytime, sugar,' said Fala as Zach turned and headed for the door.

*

After Zach had left, Wailai set her bucket of sawdust on a stool and walked up to the bar.

'You think he suspect anything?' she asked, Apache accent more pronounced.

Fala laughed. 'Just routine like he says, I'd reckon. Who cares about a loser like Whip?' She paused, added, 'But if he starts gettin' in our way we'll have to make arrangements.'

'Lawdogs make me nervous. They are cheap tippers, too.'

'Don't fret on it. He probably won't come back.' She cast a glance at the batwings, a contemplative look edging on to her harsh features. 'Everything set with Sage for tonight?'

'She did a lot of screaming until we gave her enough laudanum to take down a horse – she must be used to it.'

'This time be a little more thorough and make sure we are not interrupted.'

Wailai nodded and went back to her sawdust bucket while Fala let her gaze wander back to the batwings. She didn't damn well like it that the marshal had come here to question her about Whip Foley, though she rightly expected it. She hoped he wouldn't become a problem, though she knew eventually she would have to do something about him if her plans were to succeed.

With a laugh she uttered a mocking line: 'Listen closely and you shall hear of the final ride of Zach Revere. . . .'

Wailai glanced at her, a puzzled look in her dark eyes and Fala smiled a devil smile. She laughed again and an insane lilt danced with the sound.

*

Zach lowered himself into his chair and tossed his hat on the desk. He wasn't sure quite where to go with Whip Foley's murder, if anywhere at all. A nagging voice told him Indians weren't about to raid Carajo. It looked like just another unsolved death to be lost in the annals of the West and preserved in cheap novels such as the kind Bateman wrote. No one in Carajo would care what happened to a no-good hardcase gambler, though he reckoned Bateman's readers would after he dressed it up with a pack of lies. Despite the missing boots and unsliced clothing, it was probably just another routine killing in these parts. The scalping angle made it peculiar, but he doubted he'd be able to convince Potter it was worth wasting time on.

His questions at the Rusty Spur had turned up nothing to dispel that theory. Whip had likely gotten liquored up and taken home a dove, or at least tried to. Then he'd had gotten bushwhacked somewhere along the trail, maybe by the dove herself since she hadn't returned to the Rusty Spur.

So why couldn't he just let it go?

Because his inner sense voice was nagging him again, telling him for once he had something as marshal that wasn't routine and made him feel useful.

'*Revere!*' yelled a voice as the door burst open and Mayor Potter stormed in. Zach looked up, feeling his belly cinch.

'Yeah, Pa?' A smug look crossed Zach's features.

'I'm not in the mood, Zachary Taylor Revere. Certainly not after the parley I just had me with Mr Hawkins. He didn't cotton to you creating such a fuss over Whip Foley.'

'Sorry I didn't live up to his expectations.' Zach tried not to smirk.

Potter jammed his hands into his hips. 'I want that Whip Foley case wrapped up this minute, Zachary Taylor Revere. You hear me? Mr Hawkins has more important things to have you concerned with, such as who has been stealing his stock.'

Zach should have acquiesced, but it went against his grain to make life easy for Potter or Hawkins. Fact he had a overwhelming desire to put pebbles in their boots.

'Got me a few things I'd like to check on, Mayor.'

'Jehoshaphat, Zachary! What? Tell me what you need to check on?' Potter's face turned a shade of pink Zach usually saw on plump women.

Revere chuckled. 'His boots—'

'Were missing. I know, Zachary, I know; Mr Hawkins told me. And his shirt wasn't cut. So what? He was a hardcase. Why waste time on it when you could be tracking those rustlers?'

'He was still a human being.' Zach almost couldn't believe he was saying it. He might have shot Foley himself had circumstances been different, and shed no tears.

Mayor Potter's face shaded a deeper crimson. 'Oh, posh, now, Zachary! He was a no-good gambler and hardcase whom Mr Hawkins tried to turn to a right trail out of the generosity of his heart. But you can't change a fellow like that. They always come to no good. I've seen it a hundred times before.'

'I'm not satisfied there ain't more to this. Hawkins looked scared and it ain't galldamn likely Injuns have started comin' 'round again.'

'Honestly, Zachary. Mr Hawkins has nothing to fear from anyone. I am sure it was merely the shock of finding Whip's body on his land that made him look that way. Now, dispose of this foolishness and find those rustlers for him before he decides another marshal can do better. Does that sink in, Zachary?'

'It sinks.' Zach made a vow to be half an hour late tomorrow morning.

Mayor Potter turned and stalked through the door, slamming it behind him. Revere didn't feel much like laughing anymore. Godamighty, that pompous lardball got under his hide. He was getting galldamn tired of—

'Why don't you just let it drop, Zachary? You'd make life a whole lot easier on yourself.' Buchanan had silently opened the door and stepped into the office without Zach noticing. He peered at Zach, a sympathetic look on his face.

'How'd you know?'

Buchanan laughed. 'Saw Potter red as a beet storming out of here. Look on your face when I came in would have told me anyhow. You got a hankerin' to make more out of the Foley case than Potter wants you too. Best drop it and wrap up the Foley case. This always swimmin' upstream is gonna take years off your life.'

'Already has.'

'Then why keep worryin' the same bone?' Using a forefinger, Buchanan pushed up his spectacles and lowered himself into his chair.

'Gives me something to do.'

'You enjoy the aggravation?'

'Laura takes that notion.'

'Ain't surprised. Hell, Zachary, I consider you a friend, even if you are a royal pain in the back of the britches. Take my advice and grow old gracefully.'

'Let 'em turn me into glue?'

'You know galldamn well what I mean. You ain't

ready for pasture yet, pard, not by a damn sight. Just don't make it so hard on yourself.'

Zach chuckled, despite himself. 'Awright awright, I'll try. I'll bring Potter an apple tomorrow.'

Buchanan frowned and sighed. 'Zachary, you're not taking me seriously.'

'What do you expect from an old glue?'

'You're incorrigible.'

'Am I?'

The door burst open again and Zach's belly sank at the thought Potter might have come back. Relief crossed his face when he looked over to see a dirty-faced boy of about ten stumble in. He handed Zach a slip of paper and Zach fished in a pocket, giving him a bit. 'Don't spend that on one of them dime novels, neither,' he said with a laugh.

The boy grinned and left. Zach stared at the paper then tossed it on the desk.

'Well?' Buchanan's eyebrow arched.

'Well what?'

'Aren't you going to read it?'

'My little voice is telling me it's something to do with the Foley case. Might mean Potter has fits.'

'Yeah, sure, and I'm Abraham Lincoln.'

'Come to think of it, you'd make a hell of a president.' Zach snatched up the note and opened it, glancing at the words on the page then tossing it back down.

He plucked his hat from the desk and set it atop his head, standing and heading for the door.

'What'd it say?'

'From the undertaker. Said he found somethin' on Foley I might find interestin'.' Zach flashed him a smirk.

Buchanan groaned and shook his head.

FOUR

Zach didn't go directly to the undertaker's. It had been a long morning and having downed only two cups of Arbuckle's, his belly was starting to grumble.

He stepped into the Dusty Shamrock, Millie's eatery, which seemed to stay open all hours to cater to early risers and drunk cowboys staggering late night from the saloons, lookin' to sober up a bit before they climbed into the saddle. It certainly wasn't for the delectable menu. Millie's grub was barely tolerable, and usually soaked in enough lard to give a man three days' worth of the trots.

The room was wide and comfortable with tables adorned with blue-checkered table-cloths. Sunlight streamed through clean windows and fell across the hardwood floor that Millie kept polished enough to see your face in.

Zach took a seat at the counter, and set his hat on the next stool. The cloying scents of sizzling bacon and yeasty biscuits and brewing coffee assailed his nostrils and made his belly gurgle. Since it was early afternoon, only a few lawyers in frock coats occupied tables, as well as a couple of ladies who considered themselves the height of Carajo's society, such as it was, and a dove from one of the saloons. Millie catered to anybody and everybody and since she had the only eats in town there wasn't a hell of a lot of choice. Town had more saloons than places for decent folk, Zach reckoned.

Mildred – Millie, she liked to be called and Zach obliged – gave him a smile and came over to take his order.

'What'll you be havin', me darlin'?'

'Beefsteak and mashed potatoes and Arbuckle's finest, Millie. Same as always.'

She cocked an eyebrow. 'And same as always I'm tellin' ya you'll drink Chase and Sanborn and tink the Good Lord filled your cup with Orchard. Just be tankful I'm not cookin' today.'

'Godamighty, Millie, Arbuckle's a Western man's brew.'

'Is it now?' She grinned then handed his order to the cook in the back and sauntered back over, leaning her bony elbows on the counter. Her rosy-blonde hair was piled in a tight bun atop her head and freckles dotted the angular cheekbones and sharp nose highlighting her gaunt face. Her thin lips – matching the rest of her slight frame – became a slit when she smiled.

Zach found Millie, a former hurdy-gurdy gal, attractive in a hard sort of way. From what he knew of her background – she never hesitated to bend his ear with her frets, as well as trying to pry his out of him – her life had been anything but smooth. She had spent half her teen years in a Montana dance-hall after her mother and father were killed in a Lakota raid and indulged in more laudanum than a body should. After suffering an attack of conscience she had abandoned her wily ways and ridden a stage south with the money she'd saved and opened an eatery for weary cowhands in New Mex Territory.

'Top of the day to ya, Zach?' she asked, voice edged

with wear and the beauty of an Irish sunrise. 'You're lookin' a wee bit on the sundown side today, I'm a-tinkin'.'

Zach chuckled without humor. 'I always look that way.'

Millie gave a lusty laugh. 'Just tryin' to be delicate, I am.' Her smile widened. 'I told you any time you be needin' a wee bit of upliftin' you know where me cabin is.' She winked.

'Can't say I ain't mighty tempted.' Zach wasn't lying, either. Millie had made it quite plain he was welcome in her bed anytime and made numerous half-joking offers. More than once when he started fretting about his old life he'd considered riding out to her cabin and taking a tumble. Something always held him back, something that told him he would do irreparable damage to his already strained marriage and that it wasn't worth throwing that all away for a chasing ghost.

' 'Bout as temptin' as me victuals, I'll be tinkin', but you eat 'em all the same.'

Zach shrugged, struggling to find a smile.

'Mahrnin' harder than usual?' Millie propped her chin up on her palm.

'Naw, not really. Reckon another routine case that just puts a burr in my britches, is all.'

'Whip Foley, I'll be tinkin'.'

Zach cocked an eyebrow. 'You know about it, too?'

'Zach, me darlin' I'll be knowin' ever'ting that happens in this town.' She smiled a thin smile and her eyes sparkled, brogue thickening. 'That load of blarney repahrter t'was in airly runnin' on about it.'

Zach nodded, not surprised. 'You know Whip Foley?'

Millie scoffed, rolling her eyes. 'Begorra, doesn't ever'one? Comes in here lookin' for a free cup of me coffee ever'time he staggers out of a saloon. I'm just a-prayin' he doesn't make trouble when he's here.'

'Reckon he won't be makin' trouble for anyone anymore.'

'Like to be sayin' I'm sorry to hear that, but. . . .'

'That's what I admire about you, Millie, your honesty. Ain't much of that goin' around in Carajo.'

'And I'm always a-tinkin' its me frontage you admire!' She gave a lusty laugh and indicated her flat chest by sticking it out. Zach chuckled, an honest sound. Millie had a way of putting him at ease with her lilting voice and sometimes bawdy humor – maybe that's what he enjoyed most about coming here.

'You're a hell of a woman, Millie. Many a man'd be proud to call you his wife.'

She slapped her forehead and rolled her eyes. 'And here I'm a-tinkin' about spinsterhood!' She paused and her face went serious. 'Zach, me darlin', you have that look about ya. I can tell you're headin' for the heave and ho with our fine and dandy mayor again.'

'Reckon you're right but I ain't got much of a hankerin' to spend time trackin' Hawkins's thieves, either.' He ran a hand across his chin, feeling the stubble there. 'Somethin' 'bout the way Foley was killed don't sit right, Millie. Ain't just the fact he wasn't wearin' his boots or that whoever stabbed him bothered to take off his shirt first, then put it back on like someone tried to redress him in a hurry.'

'You're not likin' the fact he was on Hawkins's land and relieved of his locks like the redskins had come a-callin' without a whoop and a holler?'

Zach nodded. 'You *do* know everything, don't you?'

She gave him a coquettish look and peered at his southern border. 'Well, not to my way of tinkin' – but I'm a-yairnin' for the day.' She flashed him a smile that would have warmed an Irish night. 'So what's your next move? I'm a-knowin' you well enough to know you won't let the bone go once you get your jaws about it.'

Zach chuckled. 'You might just know me too well.' He got another 'not to my way of thinking' look from her. 'I'm on my way to the 'takers now. He sent me a note sayin' he had somethin' I might be interested in, which will probably only serve to further complicate my life.'

' 'Takers? Ugh! And you'll be eatin' me victuals first?'

Zach grinned. 'Better'n after, I've found.'

'Lots of folks be sayin' me victuals gives the 'taker extra business!'

'Ain't you ever serious, Millie?' Zach looked at her faded blue-green eyes and saw a hint of sorrow lurking behind their hardness and gaiety.

'Not if I can be helpin' it. You'll be seein' why when you get your order.'

'Thank you kindly, Millie.'

'For what? Bein' what is commonly refaired to as a pain in the petticoats?'

'No, for makin' me feel a little better.'

'Begorra, I could be makin' you feel a lot better, me boy. . . .' She wagged her eyebrows.

'Godamighty, I swan, someday I just might shock you and take you up on that offer.'

'I'm a-yairnin' for the day!' She leaned over the counter and gave him a peck on the cheek, then waltzed off to get his order as the cook bellowed it was ready.

The steak was as tough as an old saddle and the mashed potatoes would have glued the paper to the saloon wall. The coffee was strong enough to tan hides, but Zach devoured it with gusto, realizing Millie was right about needing a sense of humor.

After Zach finished eating, he sauntered along the boardwalk towards the undertaker's. A cool breeze felt refreshing and the stench of decaying leaves mixed with the odors of dust and dung and horse sweat blended into a musky combination that wasn't as unpleasant as it sounded. He felt a mite better now, having eaten, though Millie's food tended to squat in his belly like a bag of horseshoes.

Zach reached the undertaker's, a small clapboard building a short walk from the cemetery. HUBBLY'S UNDERTAKING AND FINE CABINETS (Pay 'Fore You Go!) was painted in gold script across the plate glass window and a model casket was on display. As Zach stepped inside, a scent of old flowers, heavy perfume and some odor Zach didn't care to place assailed his nostrils and made Millie's food all the more turbulent in his belly.

Walking through an anteroom he entered the main parlor, seeing wooden boxes that ranged from fancy rosewood things to plank on display.

Not spotting the funeral man, he walked to the small back room that served as the undertaker's office and knocked. A piping voice yelled out for him to come in. Zach entered, closing the door behind him.

A squat, bearded man with a bald head and a Father Christmas belly sat behind a desk. Numerous wooden caskets in various stages of completion filled the room and a bench for woodworking ran the length of one wall. Zach saw a table used for embalming and bottles of blood-colored preservative fluid nearby, along with a large-bore needle resting on a bench. He suppressed the urge to shudder.

Calum Hubbly – everyone called him Callous Hubbly because of his indelicate nature concerning the disposal of the dead and propensity for taking advantage of the grieving, at least their bank accounts – scooped a huge spoonful of some gelatinous substance from a large wooden bowl and shoveled it into his mouth, chewing with more noise than a cow grinding its cud.

Calum had all the manners of a prize hog, Zach reckoned.

'Zachary, m'boy,' said Calum, using the fake Scots accent he affected often – along with an Irish, German and French one, all equally bad. 'Hoot, mon, what canna do ye for?'

'Please spare me the brogue.' On Millie a brogue sounded musical, on Calum it sounded as appealing as bulls in green corn time. Calum's responding giggle sounded like a horse whinnying.

'*Oui, monsieur*, perhaps zis one would please you bettair, no?'

'No.' Zach shook his head.

'In that case . . .' Calum stuck out a plump hand, 'the house could really use a double eagle for tonight's festivities, I reckon.'

'Festivities my britches! Merna'll bleed you dry sooner or later.' Zach knew Calum spent more than any man should on a sow of a bardove named Merna. Merna was damn near twice the size of Calum, which was going some, and the couple had a love-hate – mostly hate in Zach's estimation – relationship that had resulted in Merna spending time in the hoosegow for pummeling the Jesse out of Calum one night he was a little short on greenbacks.

'She's a fine lass, m'boy.'

'Not exactly what I'd call her. She'll bury you one of these days, pardon the expression.' Zach sighed and dug into his pocket, fishing out the double eagle he'd stuffed there before entering the parlor, knowing

Calum's proclivity for wrangling money away from Zach in exchange for information. With eager fingers, Calum snatched up the coin, biting it, then stashing it in his smock pocket.

'Bless ye, m'boy, bless ye. Now what tis it you'd have me do ye for?'

'You sent a note sayin' you had somethin' on Whip Foley I might find interestin'. . . .'

'Oh, yeah, that I do, that I do.' Calum scooped up another spoonful of brownish lumps and broth and crammed it into his mouth. Half of it went into his beard. He tried to wipe it on his smock sleeve, but didn't quite get it all.

Zach stared at him. 'What the hell is that anyway?'

Calum grinned. 'Brains, m'boy, brains. Finest sonofabitch stew Millie can make.'

'Show me what you found,' Zach said, sorry he had asked and feeling his belly twist.

'Ach, yah, und if you vill just follow me. . . .' Calum extracted his bulk from the seat, no easy feat, and waddled across the room to a simple plank coffin, yanking the lid up. Zach followed.

'Hell and tarnation!' Zach blurted as an ungodly stench filled his nostrils.

'Bit short on ice lately.' Calum grinned. 'You get used to the stink after a spell.'

Zach didn't think so. The stench of rotting innards made the stew smell heavenly in comparison. 'Why the hell didn't you just embalm him?'

Calum scoffed. 'Please, Marshal, embalming fluid costs over three dollars a gallon. Bad enough I had to waste a four-dollar casket on the likes of him. Normally wouldn't even keep 'im around but I reckoned you might want to take a look at somethin'.'

Zach bet it had more to do with the fact that Calum

had a habit of going over corpses for things thieves might have missed. And with the fact that he was known to pry out gold, silver or porcelain teeth and find the most lucrative way of disposing of them. Real teeth he plucked out and sold to dentists.

Calum jerked back the hide blanket covering the body of Whip Foley. Whip, now naked, didn't look any better than the first time Zach had seen him, this morning at the Double H. The wound was a gory chasm, its edges pulled back, and the hardcase's spongy form had taken on a blanched color and still had the 'stiffness'.

'Lookie here,' Calum jabbed a finger at Whip's belly. Zach peered closely, despite his churning gut. A design showed there, burned deep into the flesh, a three-barred F; he'd seen that symbol somewhere before....

'Hell, he's been branded!' Zach looked up at the chubby funeral man.

'He's been branded awright, jest like a prize steer. Take a closer look and tell me if you've seen it before.'

Zach peered more closely at the symbol, again struck by a feeling of familiarity....

'The Rusty Spur,' he said, as it suddenly came to him. 'I saw this on their floor.'

'Uh-huh. It's on the ceilin', too. It's also at the Golden Parasol and the Silver Saddle.'

Zach peered at Calum. 'What is it? I've seen all the local brands and this ain't one of them.'

'Not sure, but I think it might belong to some secret thing – purely a guess, you understand.'

Zach nodded, wondering. 'Why the tarnation would someone brand him before killin' him?'

Calum shrugged, his mounded shoulders almost swallowing his head. 'Your guess is as good as mine.' He pulled the cover back over Whip's body, then he banged the casket lid shut.

'That it?' Zach asked.

'Yah, *mein herr*. You vant un miracle or zomezing?'

'For once, that would be nice.'

Zach left the undertaker's and Calum, who had gone back to his sonofabitch stew, and returned to his office. Sitting himself at his cluttered desk, he leaned back in his chair, balancing on two legs.

'Well?' Buchanan asked, looking up from the dodgers before him. 'Calum the ghoul have anything for you?'

'Reckon he did this time.'

'Not just an excuse to squeeze double eagles out of you, huh?'

Zach snorted. 'He still got one. Reckon Merna'll have the last say on how he spends it.' Zach paused, brow crinkling. 'Hell, I can't make no sense of it.'

'Outta what?'

'Whip's body had been branded.'

Buchanan's eyebrows arched. 'Branded? On top of bein' stabbed and scalped?'

Zach nodded. 'Told you it don't make sense. But it gives my trail sense a whole new reason to nag.'

'Why?' Buchanan folded his arms.

' 'Cause when I was at the Rusty Spur this morning I saw the same brand on the floor. Calum says it's on the ceiling there and in all the saloons.'

'He would know ... but so what? Maybe if some Apache brave did get ahold of Foley he wanted to mock the whiteman.'

'Ain't the Apache way. The scalpin' might be but I ain't never known one to brand a man and dress him back up. Had me a notion this morning somethin' wasn't right about this killin', now I've got a strong pain gnawin' my innards.'

'Probably that lousy grub you get at Millie's.' Buchanan shook his head, face growing serious. 'I dunno about you, Zachary. Sometimes I take the notion you go lookin' for trouble.'

'Sometimes it comes lookin' for me.'

'Not galldamn hard.'

Zach ran his finger across his upper lip and Deputy Buchanan went back to his work.

Zach pondered the brand on Whip Foley's body, wondering what it meant. He reckoned if Injuns had something to do with the hardcase gambler's death it was in a roundabout way. In all his years as a manhunter he had never seen the like and something about it set his blood to running, put life in his veins. Maybe this was just what he needed, to let the chasing ghost catch him, ride the trail one more time.

'Tell Potter I won't be back today.' Standing, he eyed the deputy then went towards the door.

Buchanan looked up, shaking his head. 'Mayor ain't gonna cotton to you skulkin' off so early.'

'Mayor's britches are cinched too tight anyhow. Besides, no choice. My day to fetch the boy at school. Tell Potter I'll try to bake him a pie for bein' so understandin'.'

'He'll throw it at you.'

'Reckon he will at that.'

The autumn night was frigid, crackling with the crisp fragrance of old leaves and ponderosa pine. A hazy moon beamed frozen light from an onyx sky speckled with silver spur stars. A chill breeze whispered through the two-inch window opening in Zach's bedroom, ruffling the curtains. He preferred it that way: brisk. Of course Laura didn't – Godamighty, he swore she was cold even in ninety-degree New Mex heat.

Zach lay in the darkness, hands tucked beneath his head beneath the down pillow, staring up at the vague outlines of shadowy shapes playing across the ceiling. It was well after 1 a.m. when he heard the buggy pull up, then the front door close and the receding of hooves; Laura was just getting home.

Zach caught the furtive sounds of his wife trying to be quiet and contemplated faking sleep to avoid one of her 'talks'. Why did women always want to 'talk'?. What it always came down to was a session of nobody understanding nobody, sometimes raised voices, always hurt feelings, and nothing really accomplished.

He saw a wedge of dull light as the door creaked open, then watched it disappear as the door closed. Laura undressed in the dark and softly slid beneath the cool bed covers beside him. He felt her shiver and turned his head to see her staring at the ceiling, which seemed to be something of a pastime with them.

'I thought you'd be early tonight,' he said, forging the formalities.

'Hawkins promised some fittin's to some ladies for the cotillion and there were last-minute alterations. Kept me busy for hours and I lost track of time.'

'Reckon that happens to the best of us,' he said without humor.

'Zach, are we drifting apart?' That was Laura, always to the point. Himself? He liked to beat around the old bush until something was rousted out. The direct approach sometimes felt like a knife, at least with his feelings.

'I honestly don't know.'

She turned her head towards him, her big eyes soft and pleading in the darkness. 'Zach, we can't work things out if you don't tell me how you feel. I've tried to be understanding. . . .'

'Tarnation, Laura, when? When we see each other in passing? When we lie as man and woman once a year?'

'Please don't be that way. You know why things are the way they are. It's just for a little longer.'

'I know: the house, the lifestyle to which we've grown accustomed' – or maybe the boredom to which we've become accustomed, he really wanted to say, but there was that galldamn bush again.

'Things will change, Zach. When we get comfortable. . . .'

'What? You'll quit workin' for Hawkins? I'll quit workin' for him? I reckon that ain't about to happen, Laura. Is it?'

'I don't know. Not now, maybe. But I think after we pay off the ranch—'

Christamighty, we can find some place else, move on instead of this place. Anything would be better'n to be beholden to that scalawag.'

Laura's tone went as chilly as the night air. 'What would we do, Zach? Keep on movin'? Drag Billy across New Mex, maybe Texas or some other corner of the West?'

'I don't see why not. There's gotta be somethin' better'n bein' settled here—'

'Oh, lordy – what? I swan, Zach, you don't have a lick of sense sometimes. This isn't the old days when you could just hire out to some cattlemen's association and wander off for months on end, maybe get yourself killed and leave me a widow. I can't live that way. I can't live without knowin' from day to day whether I'll be buryin' you and raisin' a son on my own. Lordy, Zach, I want another child too and once we get this ranch working—'

Zach let out a grunt. 'You honestly think Hawkins will let us even after it's paid off? Hell, the man's got a hankerin' to be bigger than Chisum. He ain't about to let some little outfit get in the way whether you're workin' for him or not. And tarnation, we're gettin' a might old for more young'ns, ain't we?'

'I got time, Zach.' Her voice came lower and he felt a surge of regret in his belly.

Zach shook his head. 'A man's got needs, Laura.'

'I've got needs, too, Zach.' Her voice softened in the still darkness. 'We need to hold on a little longer. Our relationship has to be strong enough to get through the rough times.'

His stubborn streak set in. 'Quit workin' for that man. We can't get past 'em with you always there.'

'I can't, Zach. And you can't be the man you used to be. We've both had to make changes and sacrifices.'

Zach felt his innards cinch and knew she was right. The past was gone and he was no longer a young buck on the trail and galldamn if everything in his life didn't remind him of such. What would they do if she quit working for Hawkins and they moved on to – where? Hell, he didn't even know and would have never given it a thought in the old days. But now, with Billy and responsibilities . . . a man needed roots, his pa always used to say. A man needed a place to call his own and God smite the fella who tried to take it away from him.

Was Hawkins taking Laura?

No, not really. Though it goaded him to know she worked for a man such as him, Hawkins had little to do with the fact Zach and Laura had drifted apart. Zach's own restlessness was causing that, but lordamighty Hawkins made a perfect focus for his ills.

They lay there in the silence, the icy breeze making a soughing sound as it blew through the window. He felt Laura shiver next to him again and wanted to take her in his arms the way he had when they first courted, hold her, but blamed if he could force himself to make the move.

'Have you been with another woman, Zach?' Laura asked suddenly. Zach felt himself tense, recollecting all the times he'd thought about it.

'No,' he mumbled, wondering why she had asked, but afraid to probe her.

'Would you tell me?'

'No,' he said honestly. Silence, then the creaking of the door as Ollie pushed it open and the soft padding of cat feet as he came towards the bed and hopped up. Zach stroked his ears, the cat purring contentedly, and waited for Laura to say something. She didn't. Soon her heard the steady rhythm of her deep breathing and knew she was asleep.

Zach lay there, cat nestled beside him, his mind cluttered with notions and his heart heavy.

He loved Laura. He loved her not. No, he reckoned he did. Didn't. Why was he so conflicted? Why was he so unsatisfied with things that would make a normal man turn handsprings?

Lord only knew.

FIVE

The next day Zach had still come no closer to piecing together the truth – if there was a truth – about Whip Foley.

He hoisted his feet on to his desk and leaned back, balancing the chair on two legs, hands clasped behind his head. So far, he had discovered little to go on, even with Calum's information. He had a body belonging to a hardcase gambler and drunk who had been bushwhacked and robbed, stabbed to death and scalped. And he had some peculiar brand that matched the ones on the floor and ceiling at a saloon run by a gone-to-seed whore. So?

So what?

The door burst open and Mayor Potter came through with a glare that made Zach wish he'd gone home early. '*Revere!*' the barrel-chested man yelled.

With the yell Zach almost toppled backward in the chair. He had stayed late at the office, not anxious to get home and go through another round with Laura and had assumed the mayor had gone to bed hours ago.

'Get your feet off the desk this instant, Zachary Taylor Revere. You know how much I despise that.'

Zach knew.

He swung his boots off the desk and wished he could crawl under it. He felt in no mind to deal with Potter right now.

'What in tarnation you doin' here this hour?' He frowned, voice flat.

'I got rousted out of bed by Luis Fuego, Hawkins' *segundo*. You are simply not doin' your job, Zachary. Whoever's after Mr Hawkins's stock has been at it again and stolen three horses and a handful of steers.'

Zach gave an unconcerned shrug. 'Reckon he should post more guards.'

Potter's face reddened and now that he looked more closely at the man Zach saw puffy dark pouches under the mayor's eyes. The mayor hadn't been getting a lot of sleep and that almost made Zach feel better, though he knew most likely it was because one of the local doves was keeping the portly politician entertained nights.

'I'll take a look in the mornin'. Reckon I best be gettin' home 'bout now.'

A sly expression crossed the mayor's face and Zach felt something in his belly cinch. 'Just hold your horses, Zachary. I want you to take yourself out to the Double H and meet Hawkins and his men there.'

Zach grumbled. 'Over horse and cattle stealin'? Hell, I can't do nothin' 'bout that this time of night.'

'Zachary Taylor Revere, need I remind you you are a duly sworn marshal?'

'No, but reckon you will anyway.'

Potter's sly expression got stronger. 'This has nothing to do with tracking sign, if you must be difficult.'

'You just said—'

'I know what I said, but there's also been another killing.'

'What?' Zach's face turned serious.

'Well, it seems whoever stole his stock left another body on his property, this time a woman.'

'Reckon you just got my interest, Mayor.'

Potter frowned and his brow furrowed. 'I was half afraid I would.'

The night was cold as a witch's tit and the moonlight glared like a chunk of yellow ice from the star-crystalled sky. As Zach drew Gerty to a halt near five men standing holding lanterns at the edge of the Double H spread, he dismounted then walked towards the men, the three hands and Hawkins, plus the reporter, Bateman, who scribbled on his pad.

Zach eyed the man, a frown turning his lips. 'You here again?'

Bateman grinned, looking corpselike himself under the lantern light. 'Why, yessir, I am writing a novel about the ranch. I want things to be accurate and Mr Hawkins was kind enough to have one of his men ride out and wake me.'

Zach scoffed. 'I reckon accuracy ain't got much to do with what you write.'

'Criticize all you want, Marshal, but I assure you I will portray all involved' – Bateman narrowed his gaze on Zach, the implication clear Zach was not going to come out looking good in fictional form – 'as accurately as possible.'

'I reckon,' Zach said with as much sarcasm as he could muster. Zach glanced over at the covered body – another buffalo-hide blanket – then at Hawkins, whose fear was plain as teats on a cow. Whoever was striking at the Double H was making Hawkins sweat more by the minute, perhaps closing in, and Zach couldn't help feeling a glimmer of satisfaction at it.

'You know the girl?' Zach nudged his head at the body.

Hawkins shook his head. 'Don't know her and don't care to. Just get rid of her and find out who's stealin' my stock.' The last part was delivered half-heartedly, with none of the authority Zach would have expected from a man who really wanted answers.

'You're just a bundle of compassion, Hawkins.'

'I didn't get where I am bein' charitable, Marshal.'

'No, I reckon you didn't.' Zach paused then looked at the other men. 'Any of you know her?'

One of the men's gaze darted to Hawkins, who nodded slightly, then back to Zach.

'Her name was Sage. She was a dove at the Rusty Spur.'

The revelation didn't surprise him; he had suspected who the body belonged to the moment Potter had told him it was on Hawkins's spread. The dove whom Whip Foley left with was now dead, which meant she likely hadn't killed him.

Zach knelt, bracing himself and pulling the blanket back, glancing over the body under the frigid illumination of lantern lights. He shivered, a feeling of emptiness washing over him. She was nude; the killer had not bothered leaving uncut shirts to explain this time. The wound in her chest was something that made Zach's belly knot and she had been given the same Injun haircut as Whip.

He pulled the blanket back further, scanning her smooth belly, gaze focusing on the brand burned deep into her skin. The same brand he had seen on Whip Foley and at the Rusty Spur. Why did this dove, who had left with Whip, have that brand on her? Why should she be dead a day later if a renegade Indian had attacked Whip? Something didn't make sense.

'You know this brand?' Zach looked up at Hawkins, who quickly shook his head.

'Never laid eyes on it.' Something in his voice told Zach he was lying, that the rancher at least suspected what it was.

'Any of the rest of you seen it before?'

The all shook their heads.

'Undertaker found the same brand on Foley,' said Zach. 'Local saloons have it, too. Sure you men might not have noticed?' Zach eyed the hands, who shifted feet and averted their gazes. 'Reckon you have . . .'

'What the hell difference does it make, Marshal?' asked Hawkins, tone impatient.

'Maybe none.' Zach pulled the blanket back over the body.

'Then the hell with it.' The rancher spat.

He uttered a humorless laugh and straightened, eyeing the man. 'That's what I like about you, Hawkins – you wear your heart on your sleeve.' Zach turned and walked towards his horse.

'You just do your job and stop this, Marshal,' Hawkins shouted behind him. 'I don't want no more bodies on my land. You best see to it I don't have no more stock disappear, either, or I'll make sure the mayor relieves you of your duties.'

Zach laughed without humor and climbed into the saddle. 'Hell, don't do me any favors, Hawkins. I just might start likin' you.'

The next day a blanket of gray clouds had scuttled in from the west with the threat of early snow and the air carried a chill that settled into the bones.

Zach unbuttoned his coat as he stepped through the batwings into the Rusty Spur. A piano-playing dove banged the tarnation out of the ivories on a tinkler and a willowy redhead gal was kicking up her legs and showing her unmentionables on the small stage. A few hands occupied tables.

As Zach made his way to the bar, he noticed a heavy-set Indian woman who might have given Calum's Merna competition. She had arms big as a blacksmith's. Hell, she looked like she could twist a horseshoe straight and lord knew what she could do to a man's neck. She wore a tomahawk at her waist and was dressed in a traditional Jicarilla Apache two-skin, black-tail muledeer dress sewn along the shoulders and down the sides, with fringe along the hem and a belt. Her black hair was double braided, tied with cloth strips.

The Apache gave him a cold glare and he frowned, wondering just what Fala had hired her for. Wasn't bound to be a weary hand's first choice of evening entertainment, he reckoned, except maybe for Calum, who liked 'em on the sturdy side.

Zach's gaze went to the bar where he saw Fala, dressed in her habitual red sateen bodice, wiping out a glass. The 'breed dove stood close by, checking the liquor stock. Fala turned and Zach caught that predatory look in her eyes again, but she quickly hid it.

'Why, Marshal Revere, isn't it?' She set the glass on the counter.

'Right honored you'd recollect.'

'I never forget a fella, sugar. Comes in mighty handy in my line of work.'

'Which is?' Zach asked half-jokingly, half-probingly.

She studied him, as if weighing the question for hidden intent. 'Barkeepin', of course. What all did you think?'

'Hornswogglin', maybe,' said Zach, breaking his

usual around-the-bush philosophy.

'Why, Marshal, I run a respectable saloon. A place where hands can come to relax after a hard day's toil, and engage in a few simple pleasures.'

'That what they're callin' bought and paid for sin nowdays?'

Fala let out a gusty chuckle. 'Marshal, you can't fool me. I'll just bet you've been in many a saloon in your time.'

'Reckon you might be right.'

'But I reckon you didn't come here to take up with one of my gals or whet your whistle, did you?'

Zach grinned. 'Well, reckon you're right. I have some bad news for you.'

'Hell, don't hold it till Christmas, sugar.' Her gaze drilled Zach, unflinching.

'Your gal Sage won't be comin' into work anymore.'

'No?'

'Found her body on Hawkins's land last night. She was murdered, same way as Whip.'

'Why, Marshal, I'm shocked, truly I am.' She didn't look it, Zach noted. In fact, she looked almost too calm, as if she had already known. 'You reckon that gent Foley was responsible?'

'Reckon not. She died after him, a day after looks like.' From the corner of his eye, he saw the 'breed dove glance at him, then quickly avert her gaze.

Fala's eyes hardened. 'Downright shame, but gals come and go, Marshal, 'specially the type who work for me. Reckon it makes me no nevermind. Now is there something else I can do ya for? I've got customers with dry whistles comin' in to tend to.'

Her tone had turned decidedly frigid and Zach knew there was nothing more to ask her.

'Reckon that's all I came here for. If you should hear

anything that might help . . .'

'You'll be the first to know.'

I doubt it, thought Zach. Tipping his hat, he turned and headed towards the door, suddenly stopping to gaze at the symbol on the floor, the same symbol that had been branded on to both bodies. He considered asking Fala about it but reckoned it would do no good. With a sigh, he walked out, tugging his collar to his chin to stave off the cold that had suddenly welled in his innards.

'What do you think?' asked Wailai after Marshal Zachary Taylor Revere had left the saloon.

Fala let a wry grin spread across her lips. 'I have me the notion our dear marshal suspects somethin', but he's not sure what at this point.'

'What do we do?'

'Why, sugar, we see to it, that he doesn't become any more suspicious.'

'If he does?'

'Then we'll cure his suspicion permanently.' Fala stared at the batwing doors a moment, then turned to Wailai. 'Let's take some precautions. See if our dear marshal has any family.'

Wailai smiled, an expression laced with cruelty.

The Silver Saddle was at the opposite end of Main Street and jammed between a lawyer's office and a gunsmith's. The establishment was owned by a gent named Morgan Hannely, a transplant from back east, and Zach had wasted an hour checking through wanted posters in case the man had a dodger on him, but found nothing. There was some suspicion the owner had knifed a man for not payin' for a drink but the former marshal had never been able to prove it and three witnesses – all working for the fellow – swore to it the stuck fellow had gone for his gun and Hannely had merely defended himself. 'Course the fellow was dead as a can of corned beef so he had no say in the matter.

Zach tensed as he walked through the doors. The place was dimly lit with low-turned lanterns and a gauze of Durham smoke hung in the air. The first thing he noticed was the design painted on the tiny stage – a design that was all too ubiquitous lately.

Suppressing the urge to shudder, Zach pulled his gaze from the three-barred F and gave the interior the once-over. He saw more patrons here, but of course it was later in the evening. The owner had not bothered to decorate the room; it was simply a bar with bare walls with no paintings and old sawdust on the floor. The felt was torn on a number of tables.

Zach threaded his way to the bar, pulled out a stool and sat. The bartender, a burly man with what looked to be a fake eyeball, shuffled over.

'What's your poison, gent?'

'Tell Morgan Hannely I want a parley with him.' He pulled his coat flap back flashing the tin star and making sure his Peacemaker showed clearly.

The bartender grunted. 'You're lookin' at him. I don't like lawdogs.' Morgan Hannely lived up to the front part of his name; he looked like a pirate. A gold earring dangled from his ear, and a black beard laced with streaks of gray bushed from his chin.

'I'll strike you from my Christmas list in that case.' Zach paused, eyeing the man. 'You know either Whip Foley or a dove named Sage?'

The barkeep cast Zach an annoyed glare, then sighed. 'I seen Foley in here a few times. The dove, I got no idea, mate.'

'They're both dead.' Zach said it plain, hoping for a reaction.

'So?'

'How 'bout Fala? Reckon you know her.'

'I know all my competitors – and my enemies.'

'Would she have any reason to harm either of them?' He asked it on a whim and the 'keep didn't so much as miss a beat.

'Fala ain't got no reason to harm nobody, 'cept maybe nosy marshals.'

Zach grunted, wishing he could just go back to his manhunter days when he got information at the business end of his Peacemaker.

Zach eyed the burly barkeep, brow furrowed. 'Much obliged for your hospitality.' He pushed himself off the stool and headed out, throwing a glance at the symbol on the stage before leaving. He heard Hannely cuss behind him.

The Golden Parasol was a number of notches higher on the class scale than the other saloons as far as Zach was concerned and located at the south end of town, not far from the undertaker's. The exterior carried a vaguely French look with paintings of can-can girls twirling parasols dancing across the sign. The proprietor's name was Juke Benedict. Zach wandered in around 12.30 a.m., feeling sleep begin to pull at the corners of his eyes and wondering if he weren't just avoiding going home to another round of jawing with Laura. Tarnation, sometimes he made things worse on himself, and just after complaining they weren't spending enough time together.

The sawdust was new and the lights blazed brightly from the wall lamps and a chandelier. A piano player hit the keys with considerably more finesse than the dove at the Rusty Spur. The bar looked polished as a lawyer's slicked-back hair and behind it was a gilt-framed mirror and hutches stocked with whiskey.

A pretty dark-haired girl in a peek-a-boo blouse stood near the door and as he walked in Zach couldn't help noticing her. She looked a mite older than her years, he reckoned, but it didn't detract from her looks. When he noticed her looking at him, he averted his gaze, feeling uncomfortable for no reason he could pinpoint.

Zach sidled up to the bar, gaze freezing on the peculiar three-barred symbol carved into its dark wood. He stared at it a moment, then sat on a stool.

'What'll you have?' the bartender's voice came.

'You Juke Benedict?' Zach asked the somewhat prissy looking man.

'Huh-uh, Juke's in the back with one of the girls.'

'Mind fetchin' him?' Zach showed his badge. The barkeep appeared unimpressed, but went for Juke anyway.

Juke Benedict smelled something like a polecat. Zach couldn't be sure whether the man normally smelled that way or if he were wearing some piss scent cologne. Whichever it was, Zach felt the urge to recoil the moment the man stood next to him.

Juke Benedict, though he had the classiest saloon in Carajo, was probably the sleaziest owner of the bunch. He had a reputation of never meeting a man he wouldn't back-shoot, but nothing that could be proven enough to earn him a necktie party. His ribbony hair was parted in the middle and his bushy mustache drooped over his lips. His small eyes fixed on Zach with a disgusted look.

'Whatta you want?' His tone was challenging and

Zach matched it note for note.

'You know Whip Foley or a dove named Sage?'

'Don't rightly give a galldamn if'n I do. If you ain't gonna drink, get out. I got a business to run.' Juke started to walk away.

Zach raised his eyebrows, feeling more irritated by the moment. 'I got me two killin's to figure out. Maybe a night in the hoosegow would loosen up your memory?'

Juke stopped and turned, a scowl twisting his lips. 'I ain't got no interest in no killin's, Marshal. You lookin' to pin somethin' on somebody you go somewhere else, preferably straight to Lucifer hisself.'

Zach held his ground. He saw a slight note of worry in the man's eyes, despite his talk. 'You haven't answered my question.'

Juke looked as if he were considering it. 'Hell, Whip Foley, everybody knows 'im. Don't know the dove, but I reckon I seen too many gals come and go to recollect names.'

'Know why anybody would want to kill either of them?'

'Know a hundred reasons why Whip would be put boots up. The dove, reckon I dunno. Can I go now, Marshal?' The last was said with as much open contempt as Juke seemed capable of.

Zach sighed. 'Reckon you might as well. I know where to find you—'

'Don't bother.' Juke turned away and walked through a door into the back, already pulling his shirt out of his trousers. Zach didn't have to guess what he was doing with the dove back there. He noticed, however, the door remained opened a crack, but it was too dark to tell whether anyone was watching.

Zach moved away from the bar, noticing the dark-haired girl had left the bar-room. He felt slightly disappointed the dove wasn't there and cussed himself for what he was thinking about her.

The night was downright freezing, wintry, as Zach walked down the boardwalk towards his horse, which was tethered at his office. The chill bit into him and the night had a lonesome feel to it he didn't care to think about.

'Marshal!' a girl's voice called from behind him and he stopped, turning.

He saw a woman rushing towards him, high-laced shoes clamping on the boardwalk, though by the awkward way she ran she was obviously trying to be quiet about it.

'Can I help you, ma'am?' Zach cocked his head, squinting to try to get a better look at her in the cold moonlight.

The girl stopped, out of breath and Zach got a look at her face. It was the pretty dark-haired dove he'd taken an interest in at the Parasol.

'Reckon you might.' Her voice came between sharp breaths. 'Or maybe I can help you, Marshal. I saw you show the barkeep your badge at the saloon and talk to Juke, so I hurried up and snuck out the back. They won't miss me.'

'Zach Revere,' he said, extending his hand. She took it and he couldn't deny the shimmer of heat that rippled through him.

'April, April Showers. Is there some place we can talk? I mean, I'd rather not be seen openly on the street.' Zach noticed a vague look of worry in her eyes.

'Reckon. I was just about to get a cup of coffee and a beefsteak at the Dusty Shamrock.'

'That'd be right nice.'

They walked towards the Shamrock in silence, Zach

wondering how bad Millie would tease him for bringing a dove into her eatery at this time of night.

SIX

'April Showers?' Zach gazed up from his cup of Chase & Sanborn, peering intently at the dark-haired girl. Her hair was done in large ringlets, tumbling to each side of her face. She had slipped off her cape to reveal the peek-a-boo blouse and Zach had all he could do not to stare. A thought crossed his mind: if he were going to fall for another woman, this dove would be the one. Maybe because more than anything she reminded him of what used to be, the freedom, the vitality, the fever of life surging through his veins.

'It's only my workin' name. A lot of the girls change their names when they start sellin' favors. Reckon it somehow makes it better, maybe makes a body someone else who don't have to answer to their shame.' She uttered a small laugh, one blemished with a note of pain. 'Anyway, my real name is April Snodgrass – not very exciting, is it?'

Zach shrugged. If he had to pick one thing about her he didn't find exciting that would probably be it. 'I reckon,' he said, at a loss for words.

Millie, who stayed at the eatery twenty-four hours a day it seemed to Zach, brought his beefsteak, not missing a chance to waggle her eyebrows at him. She slid a cup of Atlantic & Pacific Tea lightened with Borden condensed milk and a tea cake in front of April, not bothering to look at her.

'You be keepin' your clothes on in here, deary,' Millie said with more than a hint of cattiness. 'I'm a-runnin' a respectable eatery.' Millie whirled and pranced away.

'Who put the burr in her saddle?' asked April. 'And how did she know what I do?'

Zach cocked his head and gave a slight smile. 'With Millie you can never tell, but I reckon she knows just about everything everybody is up to in this town.'

'I'll keep that in mind.' April took a gulp of her tea as if she were swigging a Scotch. A period of uncomfortable silence settled over them, but Zach took advantage of it to finish his beefsteak and wash it down with a couple mouthfuls of coffee.

April stared at the blue-checkered table-cloth, as if her mind were somewhere else. When she finally said something, Zach detected the smallest of trembles in her voice, the ghost of some past sorrow.

'I ain't lived a very virtuous life, Marshal Revere.'

'Zach,' he told her before he could stop himself.

April reached across the table and covered his hand with hers, forcing a smile that looked a little too practiced. '*Zach*,' she said.

'Wanna tell me about it?'

'I'd like to. Ain't used to men listenin' to me, I reckon. Oh, it ain't that all-fired interestin', mind you. Just a lot of crooked turns on a straight trail. Likely it would bore you silly.'

'Try me. I'm a good listener and I want to hear about it.' Surprisingly, he did, though, he noted with mild consternation, if Laura had wanted to jaw to him about her problems he might have yawned and switched the subject to cattle rustling.

'OK, then. When I was young my ma and pa died of the consumption and the next thing I know some sheriff was sending me to a missionary home. I ran away the first chance I got. I spent the next five years gettin' caught and runnin' away over and over, bouncin' around homes – until I developed breasts and a knack for bein' nice to men. I found out real soon that with my womanly attributes and a hornswoggling attitude a gal could make a livin' in lots of places – ain't borin' you, am I?' She looked at Zach with a hint of vulnerability, something he judged she didn't allow others to see very often, if ever. He wondered why she permitted him to see it now.

He leaned back, face placid. 'Reckon you couldn't bore me if'n you tried. This connect to what you wanted to tell me?'

'I'm workin' into it.' She leaned both elbows on the table and laced her fingers. 'I started workin' the dance-halls up Wyoming way. Spent a little time at this saloon or that.'

'Sellin' favors?' Zach asked, abandoning his around-the-bush philosophy again.

Her gaze dropped, came back up. 'I'm no virgin. If a gent acts real nice, you know, just plain treats me with respect – as much respect as you could expect in the kind of places I've worked – I might be real nice to him. A gal's gotta eat, right?'

Zach nodded noncommittally. 'I reckon it's tough to get by for a gal alone.'

'You reckon right. Takes its toll on a body, but I'm willin' to risk it. I mean, what else have I got?'

Zach didn't answer, not sure what she was looking for.

'I've been around, is what I'm sayin', Zach. I know the saloons and I know how to take care of myself.

Hell, least I thought I did.'

'You ain't so sure now?'

'No, I ain't. Some *things* are going on around here and I'm startin' to get antsy.'

Zach leaned forward, forearms on the table, curiosity piqued. 'What kind of things?'

'Reckon I don't know exactly. But there's something . . . something bad, I'm sure. Ain't never seen the like.'

'Reckon I don't catch you. You got some examples?'

She hesitated, glancing at her tea cake then back to him. 'Well, the doves.'

'What about them?'

'The way they all stick together, it's a mite peculiar.'

'Sounds pretty normal from what I've seen in most saloons.'

'I've been in more saloons and dance-halls than I care to admit, from Montana to Texas, and these gals just act different than other doves I've known. More . . .'

'Cliquish?'

'Reckon you could say that. They all live together in this place Juke owns just out of town and they don't talk much to outsiders like me. And when Juke says to do something they do it like young'ns mindin' their parents when they're afraid to get a whuppin'.'

'Any of the gals got bad habits, laudanum or some such?'

'Hell, yes! More opium than I've ever seen – Godamighty, I can't believe I'm telling you this. Six weeks ago if anyone would have asked me to talk to a marshal I'da told 'em where to go and how fast to ride there.'

'Do you trust me?'

A mischievous glint sparkled in her eyes. 'No. I've never trusted anyone since my kin died, maybe not even myself. I've heard too many honey-coated promises.'

'Then why tell me?'

'Because you're the lesser of two evils, maybe. Because I heard your name mentioned by Juke today.'

A surprised look crossed Zach's face. 'In what context?'

'I overheard him talkin' with someone. I think it might have been one of the other owners, but I ain't sure a-cause I didn't dare come out of the back and see who it was. Whoever it was was talkin' real quietlike, but Juke, he's shoutin' like his britches caught fire. I don't know why they were talkin' about you, but I heard your name mentioned more than once.'

'Reckon news travels fast in this town,' Zach muttered, suspecting Fala might have been the one to visit Juke, which meant they were suspicious of him and that they had a damn good reason to be.

'How old are you, Miss April?' Zach tried to pinpoint her age but the slightly worn look of her face made it impossible for him to tell.

'Twenty-seven years. Hell, dang near to bein' an old maid. Reckon it don't make no nevermind, though. No fancy fella would never want me this way. But I'm good at what I do. Don't know that I'd ever want to give it up, but I won't lie and tell you I haven't wished for better things. Someday I might want young'ns.'

Zach studied her eyes, again seeing the vulnerability bleeding through. He had the urge to reach out to her, take her and hold her, but he knew if he did there might be no way to stop himself from going too far. It disturbed him that the urge felt so powerful, that he suddenly needed the touch, the warmth of another woman.

He fought to pull his mind from the thoughts, but

found it nearly impossible. 'Reckon many a man would want himself a wife like you, Miss April. Maybe you're sellin' yourself a mite short, if you'll pardon the expression.

She gave a derisive laugh. 'You reckon? I don't. To them I'm only good for some soft whispers and a good wick-dippin'. They don't want nothin' more and I don't ask 'em for it.' Sadness drifted into her eyes and it wasn't that far away from what he felt himself, that longing for something that wasn't any longer, could never be, for her had never been. But there was a major difference: he had Laura and April had no one, might never, since most fellas would see her as soiled goods.

'Reckon you might want to give that more thought, ma'am. Not all us menfolk got such unbending ideas and times are a-changin'.'

She gazed at him and his eyes met hers and he felt the attraction burn inside him. He had been with many a fallen women but she was different somehow. He saw tears well in her eyes, tears that didn't flow; he reckoned she was used to holding them back.

He felt suddenly uncomfortable and had an overwhelming urge to change the subject, be free of that alluring gaze. 'There's a symbol on the bar at the Parasol, like a three-barred F; it's also on the stage at the Silver Saddle and on the floor and ceiling at the Rusty Spur.'

April nodded, but made no reply.

'Got a notion what it is?' Zach prodded.

She shook her head. 'I got no idea. Always reckoned it as just carved there by whoever made the bar.'

Zach leaned back again. 'Any of the doves have the symbol on their bodies anywhere?'

Her eyes widened with surprise. 'No, not that I know of.'

'You?'

April shook her head. 'You can check me if you like....' She gave him a wink and a smile. Zach felt a shiver. It surprised him just how much he wanted to take her up on her thinly veiled invitation. He managed to smile back and ignored the remark.

'Why, is it important?' she asked.

'Reckon I don't know.' Zach hesitated. 'You know a dove named Sage or a gent named Whip Foley?'

'Reckon everyone knows Whip. Comes in often and ain't always nice to the girls. I wouldn't have nothin' to do with him.'

'The dove?'

'Name sounds a mite familiar. I might have seen her around the Parasol once or twice, but to tell you the truth the doves all start to look alike to me sometimes, so I couldn't tell you sure. Why?'

'They were both murdered. They left the Rusty Spur together and were both found on Double H land a couple days apart.'

April didn't say anything, but her face whitened.

'And they both got their hides branded with that symbol on the Parasol's bar.'

'Reckon there's somethin' else I should tell you, then, Zach.'

He cocked an eyebrow. 'What might that be?'

'Some of the gals, the ones who usually stay away from me, they kinda started makin' advances, suggestions to me.'

'What kind of advances?'

'Well, subtle ones. Like offerin' me some free laudanum or whatever I needed. One even asked if I would think of stayin' with all of them at Juke's place. I told 'em I didn't need nothin' and was stayin' at the boarding-house, but I don't reckon they're the type to take no for an answer.' She paused, her eyes taking on a vaguely frightened look. 'Reckon it scared me in a way I'm not used to bein' scared, Zach, and I ain't sure I could tell you why.'

'You reckon somethin' might happen to you if you don't come around to their way of thinkin'? Somethin' like happened to Whip and Sage?'

She nodded, the ringlets of her hair bouncing. 'Reckon that's why I made up my mind to talk to you tonight.'

Zach nodded, pondering what she had said but not sure it added up to a whole lot. Something was going on at the saloons and somehow it connected to the murders. But how? And who was behind it? One of the saloon owners? At this point he didn't know, but he did reckon it somehow connected to Hawkins and his Double H spread as well.

He finished the rest of his coffee and settled his gaze on April. 'You see anything else, or get into any trouble, you send for me, ma'am.'

'Does this mean the evenin's come to an end?' She raised her eyebrows.

'Reckon I'd best be gettin' home. I haven't got much shuteye in the past few days.' He should have said Laura was probably worrying about him now, but something held him back and he reckoned it wasn't something good.

April turned her head and stared out the condensation-beaded window. She appeared lost in thought, face suddenly blank, like a practiced mask put on to hide her feelings.

'Reckon it's gonna be a cold night . . .' she murmured.

Zach nodded, having an idea what she was hinting at, and feeling nervous because he hoped it was true.

'I'll see you home, ma'am,' he said before he could stop himself.

April turned to him, the vague sense of vulnerability washed from her features. She was a woman, now, a beautiful sensual creature who handled men like playthings and with the deftness of Circe. Strong, in command, with an armor of toughness that protected her from any chance of getting hurt. He felt that draw him in, prey on his own sense of desire for things that had been. It pried at the restlessness and urges he'd felt welling inside him over the past few months, a sweet promise that said, 'I'll take away your boredom, your pain, make you young again. I'll make you happy for a spell, but there's a price.'

His marriage.

Godamighty! What the tarnation was the matter with him? Laura and Billy were at home waiting on him, trusting him and here he was with a whore, actually taking the notion of doing something that would hurt them deeply, damage his marriage and the few morals his Bible-thumping pa had pounded into his mule-brained head. And he reckoned he didn't care.

Did he?

'I'd surely like that, Zach.' April smiled, the smile of a sorceress. She said his name as if it belonged on her lips.

Zach stood and pulled on his coat, feeling his legs go weak and his heart pound like a horse runnin' from a rattler. Why was he sweating? He rubbed his palms on his trousers, then set his hat on his head.

April stood and put on her cape, her gaze not leaving him, adding to his unease. He was glad when they headed for the door.

'Evenin', Millie,' said Zach when he noticed her staring at him, a smirk spread over her thin lips.

'Don't you be doin' nuttin' I wouldn't do,' she said sarcastically.

'Tarnation, that don't leave me much leeway, Millie.'

'More than you tink. And if you be needin' your saddle soaped, you know where I live.'

'You're incorrigible, as Buchanan would say.'

'Gosh and begorra yer right about that!'

They walked to the marshal's office in silence and Zach unhitched Gerty, who was all but asleep on her feet. Stepping into the saddle, he helped April on to the back, the feel of her front pressed to his back arousing and filling him with guilt at having thoughts he should have been having with Laura. April's body was soft and as her hands went around his belly he had all he could do to concentrate on his marriage.

How long had it been since he and Laura had been together in the Biblical sense? Hell and tarnation, too long! There never seemed to be time or either of them was too tired and then there was the chance of another child.

It would be so easy to be with April, so galldamn comfortable, a giving in to the past and the man he used to be. She was young and warm and there would be no strings attached. . . .

Godamighty! He was thinking plumb foolishness again! He did love Laura and just because things weren't right at the moment didn't mean they wouldn't change. If he weren't so mule-assed stubborn and just accepted he was no longer a manhunter on the trail. . . .

The boarding-house was a about a half-mile from the marshal's office and Zach drew up, his hands damp as they clutched the reins with the force of a drowning man clutching a log in a raging river.

'Mrs Appleby's usually a bit funny 'bout who she rents to. . . .' Zach said, wondering how April had ever convinced the old woman to give her a room.

April gave an easy chuckle. 'Mrs Appleby's also got a taste for fine Orchard and a niggardly way about her. Reckon a few bottles a week and two bits extra a night gets me a permanent place to live long as I keep her happy.'

Zach laughed and swung from the saddle, then helped her down. He walked her up to the door and she turned to him.

'You're a nice man, Marshal Zach Revere.' April's gaze lingered on him, the vulnerable child look back in her eyes. But the child was quickly spirited away in favor of the woman, the temptress.

April leaned up suddenly and kissed him full on the lips. Zach found himself responding, though something inside him didn't want to while something else did. Her lips were soft and sweet, with the vague aftertaste of smoke and tea, and he wanted to give in to them, let himself be carried away. For a suspended moment he was back on the trail again, a gal in every saloon and free of any chasing ghosts.

For only a moment.

Despite his aching desire, he forced himself to push her back, breaking the kiss. 'I'm sorry, ma'am,' he said, running his finger over his lips. 'I just can't.'

'I'm lonely, Zach. Lonely and scared. I need you to stay with me tonight. *You* need to stay with me tonight. I can read men. You're not happy and there's somethin' missin' in your life. I can make you happy. I can fill that missin' part. Least for a spell.'

'I . . .' Zach battled with his conscience; if he stayed much longer he would lose the fight. He wanted her.

Godamighty, he wanted her. But there was Billy's smiling eight-year-old face and Laura's soft blue eyes, shining, trusting. Even Ollie's furry face forced its way into his thoughts. How could he betray them and live with himself? Did it matter?

'I'd best be goin',' he said at last. He started for Gerty, his innards jumping like a bronc-buster on an outlaw horse. He heard the sound of the door softly closing, and when he looked back he saw April had disappeared into the boarding-house.

Zach unsaddled Gerty after putting her in her stall then brushed her down, thoughts still stuck on the lingering taste of April's kiss. He saw her lovely face in is mind, felt an aroused chill shudder through him. What if he *had* given in? Would it have really mattered? He felt unsatisfied with his marriage, his life. He and Laura were just drifting apart, weren't they?

But he loved Laura. Something was still salvageable in their marriage, if only he'd let himself realize that what he already had mattered more than what tempted him. How could he just throw away years of love, compassion and devotion over some horse-brained restlessness and desire to recapture his past?

'Christamighty, Gerty,' he muttered, stroking the horse's mane. 'You got a sorry old fool for an owner.'

Gerty snorted as if agreeing and Zach let out an easy laugh.

'You and me are too much alike, old girl. We both seen our better days and wish we hadn't.'

Whether Gerty did or didn't he wasn't positive but, hell, someone had to empathize with him.

Lordamighty, he felt confused. He couldn't recall

ever being this bewildered in his life. 'What happens, you hit forty and fall apart?' he asked himself. 'Gotta prove you're still worth something?'

Zach gave his head a violent shake and closed up the stall then the stable doors and headed towards the house.

He stared at a dull light shining from the kitchen and looked back at the stable, knowing he would have to spend some time cleaning it in a day or two and the restlessness burned inside him again. He reckoned April's kiss had done nothing to alleviate that in the slightest and the thought of mundane tasks merely added to it. 'Routine, Zach, you old fool. Always routine.' His words dissolved in the chilly air.

Zach made his way up the front steps and stopped short on the porch. Any thoughts of routine or April were suddenly bucked from his mind and every muscle tensed.

A knife protruded from the door, a Bowie knife, its blade driven deep into the wood. Carved into its handle was a symbol, one that made Zach's blood run as chilled as the night – the same three-barred F he'd seen branded on to the bodies of Whip and Sage.

Its blade pinned two things to the door – a note and a grisly memento that should have been hanging from a warrior's lodgepole. He stared at it for dragging moments, then grasped the knife and yanked. He had a devil of a time wrenching the Bowie loose. He pulled off the patch of hair, long and dark and Zach bet he knew who the scalp belonged to. The dove named Sage. He shoved it into a pocket, his belly turning with nausea.

Plucking the note from the blade, he opened it, straining to read the words under the poor illumination of blanched moonlight. Three lines, scrawled in over-large blocky letters:

WE KNOW WHERE YOU LIVE, MARSHAL. WE KNOW YOUR FAMILY. LEAVE US BE.

SEVEN

Zach eased the front door shut, leaning his back against it. Sucking in shallow breaths, face strained, he tried to grip his composure. The threat to his family confirmed there was more to Foley and the dove's murders than just some supposed Indian attack. Someone didn't want him poking around and it could be anybody from Hawkins to any of the saloon owners.

April had overheard Juke Benedict discussing Zach with someone and it was likely Benedict had some sort of connection to what was going on. If he had been talking to Fala, or possibly even Hannely, then they were also involved. There was also the matter of the brand – all three places had it, but what did it mean? That all owners were involved? Why would they care about a hardcase gambler like Foley? And why would one of their own girls be killed?

Zach turned the Bowie knife over in his hand, staring at the strange three-barred F carved into its handle. On impulse, he deposited the weapon in his coat pocket, along with the note. Removing his coat, he hung it on a hook in the pantry, then went through the kitchen and down the hall to Billy's room. Opening the door a few inches, he looked in, making sure his son was safe. In the dim illumination from moonlight slicing through the blinds, he saw Billy sleeping soundly, blankets pulled up to his chin.

Godamighty, he loved that boy; if anything ever happened to him....

Leave us be the note said. What if he did? Would it end the threat to his family? Or would whatever was happening grow into a bigger menace, eventually endangering them anyway?

He was the marshal and sooner or later whoever was taunting Hawkins – Zach had become almost certain that's why those bodies were dumped on Double H land – would strike with whatever they had in mind and he would be forced to act. Hawkins was not a man to sit still for it either. He had been subdued up to this point, leaning on the mayor to lean on Zach to chase down his rustlers.

Yet strangely Hawkins had not leaned on the mayor to force Zach into finding out who left those bodies. Why? Did Hawkins know why they were being left there? Did he know who was taunting him? Zach had to wonder. He had seen the fear in the man's eyes and a man like Hawkins didn't booger for no reason.

Zach could only see one way for Hawkins to go if it kept up. If he didn't want the marshal involved he would posse his own men and go after the perpetrator, take matters into his own hands. He had the power and money to get away with it too and that fact alone was enough to make Zach know he couldn't avoid his duty in finding out what was going on.

But that meant risking his family sooner rather than later and he cottoned to neither option.

Sighing a weary sigh, he softly closed the door behind him. He made his way down the hall to the kitchen, going to the blue enamel pot and pouring himself a cold Arbuckle's.

'Zach?' A sleepy Laura came from the bedroom, wrapped in a robe and rubbing her eyes. 'Why didn't you tell me you'd come home? I waited up a while but got tired and fell asleep.'

'Reckon I didn't want to wake you.' He hoped it didn't come out like the half truth it was. The fact of it was he felt guilty as hell for that kiss April had planted on him and worried about the threat. He knew Laura was smart enough to see either on his face and question him and Lord knew he was in no frame of mind for that.

'Is something wrong?' Laura seated herself at the table and wrapped her arms around herself.

'No, why?' Zach took a gulp of the strong brew in an effort to disguise his lie.

'You look a mite awful. Your face is pale, your forehead damp. Too much time at the saloons?' A wry gleam sparkled in her sleepy eyes.

Zach almost choked on his Arbuckle's. 'How'd you know I'd been to the saloons?'

'Had to go into town for a fittin' for Mrs Blevins. One of Hawkins's men brought me in. I stopped by the office and Buchanan told me you were looking into the murder of some gambler and dove from one of the saloons.'

'Good old Jess. Reckon you're jealous?'

Her face hardened. 'You know how I feel about those places. I know you spent enough time in them in your manhuntin' days but that don't mean I like knowin' it or want you there now. Too many temptations for a man like you.'

Zach felt his blood boil. 'What the tarnation's that s'posed to mean?' He said it a little too defensively, recollecting April's kiss again and hoped he wasn't giving his guilt away.

'I mean you got enough of a ghost chasing you. You certainly don't need any other reminders. Those places are full of nothin' but drunks and fallen women and sin and a decent man don't belong in them, least not a married one.'

'I'm just doin' my job, Laura. Two killin's seem to point to the saloons. I got no choice but to go in there.'

'You don't have to enjoy it!' Her eyes narrowed, accusing, and he felt himself want to shrink.

'Who said I did?' Zach countered.

'You just told me.' Laura's eyes flashed cold, probing, as if she were looking for evidence on which to convict and hang him.

Zach, after gulping down the remainder of his coffee, set his cup on the counter and leaned over the sink, staring out of the window into the frosty night.

'Laura ... has anyone been around tonight?' He didn't want to tell her about the knife in the door and the note and scalp, didn't want to alarm her unnecessarily, but he needed to know.

Laura looked perplexed. 'What do you mean, *around*? Who?'

'I mean here, at the house. Did anyone strange come to the house today?'

She shook her head. 'No, nobody. Is there something you're not telling me, Zach?'

Zach turned, looking contrite. 'No ... no, I reckon I just want you to be careful, is all.'

'I'm a big girl, Marshal' She almost smiled. 'I think I can handle myself and there's a Spencer on the parlor wall. I know how to shoot as well as any man. If there's some danger from this case you'd best tell me.'

'No, no danger. I jest don't want to take any chances that there might be, I reckon.'

'Zach, you're not making any sense. Why don't you

just tell me what's goin' on—'

'Christamighty, nothin'! Nothin's goin' on!' Zach's voice snapped out, nerves cinched from worry.

'Zach, what's in the Lord's name's the matter with you?' Laura snapped back. 'You chew my head plumb off at the least little thing. I can't even talk to you anymore.'

Zach felt defeated and seemed to deflate. 'Godamighty, Laura, I don't know what's the matter. I jest don't know. Maybe it's me, maybe it's you, maybe it's just the way everything in my life seems so stuck. The wheels are turnin' but I'm goin' nowhere but down a sundown trail – *we're* goin' nowhere.' God help him, April's face rose in his mind and he could feel her warm body in his arms.

'What are you talkin' about?' Laura's eyes hardened with a mixture of defensiveness and anger. 'I know we have things to work on, but I thought we worked this out some the other night— Godamighty, Zach, sometimes I just don't know what you want! Do you still want me? Do you want one of those whores at the Rusty Spur?' She stood and drilled him with her gaze.

'Judas H. Priest, that ain't fair, Laura!' But Zach almost wanted to scream out that he'd been tempted by April, that he was still tempted by her, just to see the hurt in Laura's eyes, just for once to get the upper hand on her in an argument. But something held him back and he reckoned he was glad.

'Maybe it isn't, but it's not fair what you're doing to me. You're not being honest, and I can't help this marriage if you won't try. I ain't one of your saloon girls, Zach. You can't just leave me and ride off in the mornin' and expect to come back whenever you got the notion. I believed you meant it when you asked me to marry you and said you wanted to give up bein' on the trail. I can't compete with a ghost and I'll be blamed if I'll even try.'

Zach felt the last of the fight go out of him, knowing she was right and damn near despising her for it. He wondered sometimes how he could be such a selfish stubborn old bastard. 'You ain't listenin', Laura.'

'Listening to what?' Laura shifted feet, mouth drawing into a tight line. 'Listening to how you wish you didn't have me and were back on the trail? Killin' men for money?'

Zach turned back to the window, leaning heavily on the counter. 'Listenin' to *me*, my needs.'

'Just what are your needs, Zach? A woman who stays home and takes care of the young'ns and the house and cooks you dinner and waits patiently by the door for you to come home at some god-awful hour after spendin' the night in a saloon? I'm not that woman, Zach. You knew it when you married me and you know it now. I want this ranch just as much as you do and if workin' for Hawkins means we'll get it faster then I'm willin' to do it.'

'That ain't what I meant and you know it.'

'Then tell me what is it you *do* mean, Zach? Tell me so I can understand.'

Zach felt anger boil because he knew he was losing. Again. And he knew he was losing because he had nothing to battle with, no legitimate ground on which to stand. He was instead sinking into quicksand and sinking a mite too fast. Laura was right – she was always right: he didn't know what he wanted. He had everything, yet nothing, and he just didn't know why he felt the way he felt, why that ghost was chasing him so doggedly.

'We ain't been together in ages, Laura.' Zach's voice lowered. 'Not since you started workin' for Hawkins.'

'Lordy, Zach, when do we have the time? If I'm not late you are, and we're both tired tryin' to keep this ranch runnin'. Soon as it's paid for we can—'

Zach spun, face livid. 'Then what? We settle down and have us a passel of young'ns? Start the whole process all over again? Maybe have to work for Hawkins even longer?'

'Zach, what difference does it make whether it's Hawkins or someone else? That isn't the problem.'

'Hell it ain't,' he said, belly cinching because he was afraid she was right.

Laura let out a prolonged sigh. 'It's you, Zach. You can't turn around and face that ghost. You best make a choice between what you were and what you are, because you can't be both. And I can't keep worryin' I'll find you with some saloon girl or just gone completely because you want your old life back. This is what you have, Zach, a wife and son who love you and want to make a home of this ranch. If that ain't enough you best let me know.' She stared at him a moment and when he didn't turn around he heard her going back towards the bedroom. When he turned she stopped half-way down the hall.

Laura sighed, a look of resignation welded onto her face. 'You always end it this way, Zach, and it gets us no further than when we started.'

Zach ran his hand through his hair. 'I'm sorry, it's as far as I can go right now. Reckon I need time to think things out.'

'Then take your time. But don't take too long because I might think things out and make a decision for you. I'm goin' to bed. Are you comin'?'

'I wanna stay up a spell.'

'Zach . . .' Laura shook her head, casting him an irritated look, then turned and headed down the hall without another word.

Alone in the kitchen, Zach felt post-fight silence crushing him. He shouldn't have treated Laura that way; she didn't deserve it. She was holding up her end of their marriage; it was him who wasn't holding up his. But the knowledge of that fact didn't do him a gall-damn bit of good.

Zach wandered into the parlor, which contained a sofa and two horsehair chairs, a pot-bellied stove and a wall rack holding a Spencer carbine. He slumped on to the over-stuffed sofa after turning a lantern low. Slipping off his boots and unbuckling his gunbelt, he draped it over a chair then curled up on the sofa. He stared up at the ceiling, watching a spider meander its way across. The spider zigzagged, appearing as if it didn't know where the hell it wanted to go but somehow managed to get there all the same. He reckoned that spider was never really confused as to its destination, it just strayed off the trail getting there once in a while.

Are you going to stay off that trail?

His mind turned to April again: twenty-seven, beautiful, inviting. A ghost of the past. He found himself contemplating what it would be like to spend the night with her, running through the pros and cons, always ciphering a heavy deficit on the pro side.

Zach's reverie was broken by a heavy ball of fur and feet that leaped up on him.

'Howdy, Ollie.' He hoisted the cat to a comfortable position by his side. 'Christamighty, you best lose some weight.' Ollie seemed unimpressed by the proclamation. The cat purred contentedly as Zach scratched his ears then suddenly took a bite out of his finger, drawing blood.

Zach let out an 'Ouch!' and peered at the cat, who had the peculiar habit of biting the hand that fed it.

Laura had told him that was the cat's way of showing affection, but Zach found it galldamn annoying – and painful. The cat peered back at him indifferently, then lowered its head and closed its eyes. Zach shook his head, thinking the cat and his life in general had a lot in common.

The next thing he knew, the sun was glaring through the windows and Billy was prodding him awake. Groggily, Zach prised his eyelids open; the brightness stung and he squinched them shut again, opening them more slowly to let them adjust to the light. He noticed his breath smelled as bad as Ollie's.

'C'mon, Pa, we're gonna to be late.'

'Aw . . . what time is it?' He noted Billy was already dressed and that was a bad sign in itself.

'Reckon it's near eight already. Ma already left for the Hawkins ranch.'

'Godamighty.' Zach heaved himself off the couch, much to Ollie's consternation, and staggered to the bedroom, going to the porcelain wash-basin, doing a quick clean-up and not bothering to change clothes. Going back to the parlor he pulled on his boots and buckled on his gunbelt. Billy was already outside, waiting with Gerty. Zach went to put on his coat and recollected the knife and note and scalp in his pocket. He pulled them out, examined them briefly then shoved them back into the coat.

He went to Gerty and mounted, swinging Billy into the saddle behind him. As they rode into Main Street, Billy did his slouching routine, hoping not to been seen by his schoolmates.

Zach would have laughed, but he felt too tired. He hoped he would wake up fully before he wandered into work.

Zach drew up in front of the school and Billy climbed from the saddle.

'Billy...'

'Yeah, Pa?' The boy looked entirely too cheerful for the early morning hour.

'Be careful, boy. Don't talk to no one you don't know.'

'Pa?' Billy looked puzzled.

'Just mind my words.'

Billy nodded and ran off towards the school. Zach watched him go, a feeling of worry mixed with a touch of sadness welling within him. He reined around and headed towards his office, praying his father's God looked out for sons of ex-manhunters.

EIGHT

Zach almost fell asleep at his desk. He had all he could do to keep his head up. The sea of paperwork and dodgers before him seemed to blur into a white and sepia ocean. Boring. Routine.

'Late night?' Deputy Buchanan, sitting behind his desk, peered over his spectacles at him.

'Reckon you could say that.' Zach rubbed the back of his neck.

'Spendin' a mite too much time in the saloons, Zachary?'

Zach managed a half-hearted laugh. 'One of the doves, April, had something for me—'

'I'll just reckon,' quipped Buchanan.

Zach ignored the remark. 'She told me things that seem to tie in with the murders of Whip Foley and Sage.'

'Judas H. Priest, that again!' Buchanan blew out a disgusted grunt. 'You still won't let that die, pardon the poor choice of words. The mayor ain't right happy with you as it is. He wants you on the Hawkins rustlin' case.'

'Don't give a diddly damn what Potter or Hawkins wants. I got a notion this case goes a whole lot deeper than I originally suspected. It might even tie in with Hawkins's missing stock.'

'Hope you're right – for your sake.' Buchanan stood. 'I'm goin' for some of them powderkeg biscuits Millie makes, you want anything?'

'Reckon I'll jest drink that swampwater you call coffee. Need somethin' to keep my eyes open.'

'Suit yourself.' Buchanan set his hat on his head and walked out into the cool morning air. Zach went back to trying to fake interest in his paperwork, but with no success. Images of April kept popping into his head, along with a feeling of longing and restlessness. He cursed himself for dwelling on her, especially in light of his discussion with Laura and the grisly warning stuck to his door. When he'd reached the office, he'd stowed the scalp, note and Bowie knife in a desk drawer, not mentioning them to Buchanan.

A sudden rattling drew his attention and his gaze lifted to a paneled wagon that had rounded the corner on to Main Street. The contraption bounced and bobbed its way along the rutted thoroughfare, kicking up dust and dried dung and looking for all the world as if it would topple over at any moment. A second smaller wagon followed on its heels, this one looking a bit more sturdy.

Rising and going to the window, Zach's gaze centered on the first wagon, which had words painted on its side in fancy rolling letters that said CAPTAIN WALLABY'S FUMADIDDLE TRAVELIN' SHOW AND CURE-ALL EMPORIUM. A wizened man in a stove pipe hat, red frock coat and a white Vandyke beard drove the horses.

A dark-haired girl snapped the reins on the second wagon which boasted JULIANKA, PSYCHIC AND PHRENOLOGIST EXTRAORDINAIRE: See All, Know All, Tell All – Two Bits! on its side.

Zach had seen a number of tinkers and snake-oil salesmen pass through Carajo and normally it little concerned him. They sold their noxious mixtures to the unsuspecting and gullible and he reckoned for the most part little harm came from it.

What concerned him about this troupe had nothing to do with possible snake-oil ingredients, but the symbol painted beneath the legend on the second wagon – a peculiar three-barred F.

He rubbed his jaw, eyes narrowing, as he watched the wagons rumble past, heading towards the town square.

The door opened, disturbing his reverie, and Buchanan, a basket of biscuits couched in the crook of his arm, came in. The deputy looked at Zach and Zach nudged his head towards the two-wagon caravan. 'You ever seen them before?'

Buchanan looked out in the street, then back to the marshal, shaking his head. 'Reckon not that one in particular, but seen plenty like it. Snake-oil salesmen come through every town.'

Zach went back to his desk and scooped up his hat, setting it on his head. He slipped into his coat and started for the door. It was Laura's day to pick up Billy so he had plenty of time.

'Where you goin'?' asked Buchanan, looking puzzled. 'I don't like that look on your face. I got a notion you're about to look for trouble.'

'Reckon I'm gonna buy me some snake oil.' Zach grinned and went through the door.

'Yes sir! Captain Wallaby's Cure-All Elixir is guaranteed to fix what ails ya! Cancer, the consumption, the gout, cholera and the plague! All of 'em turn tails and run at the sight of this magical potion, my fine folks, they surely do. For only four bits you can be cured of all your ills and live to a ripe old age!' The wizened man stood on an over-turned crate and waved an arm like a cowboy circling a lariat. In his other hand he clutched a bluish bottle Zach assumed was the 'medicine' the man was hawking.

A small crowd had gathered and were peering intently at the man, their attention captured by the rise and fall of his voice. Zach had to give him one thing: the man was a powerful speaker with a voice as silky as a lady's unmentionables. His wagon stood off to the side, horses snorting.

The second wagon was angled in front and the dark-haired girl eyed him with large brown eyes and a beckoning smile as he approached.

'You want Julianka your fortune to tell you? Perhaps your head to feel and predict, no?' she asked in a honey-coated voice punctuated with an alluring raise of her eyebrow. Her eyes looked a liquid brown and ringlets of black hair fell to her shoulders. His gaze shifted to the wagon, to the symbol painted on its side. Lingering there, he studied the three-barred F. It perfectly matched the symbols found in the saloons and on the bodies.

Zach shook his head, not taking his gaze from the symbol for a moment. 'No, reckon if I knew my future I might be afeared to get up in the mornin'.'

The girl peered at him as if not understanding his cynicism, then a beguiling smile widened on her full lips. 'Ahhh, for you good fortune and great wealth only, *signor*, Julianka predicts it. Julianka sees all.'

Zach looked at her. Dressed in a simple gypsy peasant blouse and skirt, she wore more bracelets on both wrists than he ever recalled seeing on a single person.

He nudged his head at the three-barred F. 'This symbol, what does it mean?'

The girl's expression darkened, eyes narrowing. 'You do not want to know that symbol, *signor*. It belonged to a bad woman, a very bad woman, the devil's temptress herself.' Zach noted she lost some of her gypsy accent. She shook her head, dangling moon-and-star earrings tinkling.

'Bad woman? It was here before you started telling fortunes?' He drew a double eagle from his pocket, holding it out.

The gypsy woman gave the slightest shake of her head. 'Keep your monies, *signor*. Julianka sees no more.' She held up her hands on a halting gesture and with a sharp motion whirled, bracelets clacking. She vanished behind the wagon.

Zach's gaze returned to the symbol a moment then he moved towards the crowd, who were beginning to shuffle off, each clutching a bottle of Captain Wallaby's elixir.

Zach waited until the last of the townsfolk was gone before approaching the snake-oil salesman. He saw the man counting greenbacks with a greedy look glinting in his eyes. He glanced up as Zach approached, jolting slightly, and a vague expression of worry turned his gaunt face.

'Why, Marshal, I assure you everything I said about my elixir is the God's honest truth, yes sir, it is. Cures everything from rheumatism to the collywobbles.' He stuttered a nod and with his Vandyke the man reminded Zach of a billygoat.

'You Captain Wallaby?'

'Er, Captain Wallaby met with an unfortunate accident a year back or so.'

'Accident?' Zach raised an eyebrow.

The little man nodded, stuffing the greenbacks into his pocket. 'Why, yes, er, saloon gal got the better of him after she discovered his elixir didn't take away a case of, er, well, something common to ladies of the night, shall we say – 'course, we improved it to do that, now.' He grinned.

'Who are you, then?'

'Name's Benjamin T. Barlow, at your service, Marshal.' He gave a curt bow.' We just keep the name up for recognition.'

'We?' Zach studied the man's eyes. They were small and sunk deep in his face and had a habit of never staying in one place more than a second or two.

'Julianka and me, of course. Finest psychic and phrenologist this side of the Pecos, maybe t'other side, too.'

Zach got right to the point. 'She seemed a mite skittish when I asked her 'bout that symbol on her wagon.'

A nervous light jumped into Benjamin T. Barlow's eyes. His scalp tightened like a grinder monkey's. 'Er, symbol?'

'Reckon maybe you could tell me what it is.'

'It means nothin', Marshal, just something the original owner had painted on there for decoration, I am sure. Now, if you'll pardon me I have to prepare more elixir for the next . . .'

He was lying. Zach heard it in his voice and felt a measure of irritation at the fact. As the little man turned to skitter away, Zach slammed a palm into the side of the wagon, preventing him from going.

'I reckon you know galldamn well what means. And you best tell me 'fore I lose what little's left of my patience.'

The man's eyes darted back and forth and he looked suddenly terrified. 'P-Please, Marshal, just forget you ever saw that symbol. It means nothing. It used to belong to someone who used to work for me, that's all.'

'Julianka said it belonged to a bad woman – what was this woman's name?'

Benjamin T. Barlow looked as if he might suddenly need a bottle of his own elixir to keep him from blacking out from fright. Zach grabbed two handfuls of the man's frock coat and shoved him against the side of the wagon.

'Look, Barlow, I got two murders and a threat to my family to figure out and I think this symbol has somethin' to do with it. I've seen this symbol in three saloons in town and now I see it on one of your wagons. I want to know how it got there and what the tarnation it is or you and Julianka can just spend the next few days in one of my cells courtesy of the Carajo Welcomin' Committee.'

The man's gaze finally stopped, caught by Zach's own, and he started to tremble. 'Y-you seen that symbol here in town? In the saloons?'

Zach raised an eyebrow. 'Two bodies got branded with it, gent.'

'Sh-she's here?'

'Who? Who's here?'

The man swallowed hard, his overly prominent Adam's apple bobbing. 'Fala. . . .'

The name hit Zach like a cold stream on a summer day. 'The saloon owner?'

'Hell, I don't know about that, but if she's in town I don't want to be, no sir. She's evil.'

'You best explain and do it 'fore I take a notion to bring you right to the Rusty Spur and question you in front of her.'

The man shuddered. 'No! Please. I don't want no part of her. She used to be my psychic. She fancied herself an Apache shaman, a powerful witch and hell if I don't think she was right. I use to see her dance late at night, get all dressed up in a black robe and Apache warpaint. Scared the beejesus right on out of me. That was her symbol.'

'For what?'

'She got visions, she told me, visions of having a town all to her own, setting herself up as some kind of great Injun queen, she said, and makin' some fella pay for what he did to her.'

Zach's gaze narrowed. 'That symbol's her initial?'

'Yep, she said it was her brand for her spread when she took over some place – the Bar F, she wanted to call it. I told her there ain't no cattle queens and she was spittin' in the wind if she thought there ever would be but she got powerful angered about it and trounced me half to hell and back. Day she left she said she ever laid eyes on me again she'd cut my scalp off and feed it to the buzzards.'

The revelation hit Zach with a chill. 'The two folks who got murdered, they were scalped. . . .' His voice trailed off.

'Don't surprise me none. She's part Apache, her ma was a squaw whose husband beat the hell of her for havin' an affair with a local ranch-hand. Fala came outta that union and the husband never accepted her as his own. Reckon he hated even lookin' at her. One day he beat her ma harder than usual and left her for dead with Fala cradling her in her arms. She was only ten. The mother survived a spell but wasn't never the same and one day the man came back and shot her brains out. Apparently didn't want no chance of it ever bein' found out.'

'What happened to her after that?'

'She said she ran away and lived with the Apaches a

spell, then she started workin' in a few saloons and plannin' her revenge on the man who killed her ma. Said she wanted to bring the Apache back to their full glory, start a new era of redskin rule, only this time by squaw warriors.'

Zach's eyes turned thoughtful. 'You hired her knowin' this?'

The man squirmed. 'Hell no! I hired her 'cause she was dark enough to pass herself off as a gypsy and claimed the Injun spirits told her folk's futures. I didn't know she was plumb loco till she got drunk one night and started blabbin' 'bout her plans. Reckon she didn't even recollect the next morning what she'd told me and I wasn't about to bring it up. When she pulled stakes I did a jig, Marshal, I swear I did.'

Zach studied the man, deciding he was telling the truth. It convinced him Fala was somehow involved with Whip Foley and Sage's murders. But why? What did either of them have to do with her plans to create an empire for herself, re-establish the Apache?

Zach let go of the man's coat and sighed. 'I reckon you better take your wagon back on the trail, Mr Barlow. We got enough snake oil in this town to last us a lifetime.'

Barlow looked relieved. 'I plan to, Marshal, by Jehoshaphat, I surely do.'

After the marshal walked away Benjamin T. Barlow gave in to a prolonged case of the shivers, then, getting himself under control, scurried around the wagon and bellowed at Julianka to get ready to pull out. He had no desire to be within a hundred miles of Fala, not now, not ever.

He yanked a bottle of his elixir from his pocket and uncapped it, gulping a deep drink. It was a downright noxious blend of snake-head whiskey, molasses, Arbuckle's and boiled trough water but it was the only spirits he had at the moment and he wasn't about to go spend his greenbacks in a saloon the way he usually did if Fala owned them. 'Jehoshaphat!' he blurted, wincing as the elixir seared its way down his gullet. 'Good for what ails ya, my buggy-bruised britches!' he muttered and turned.

His heart clawed its way into his throat and he froze, a wave of panic surging through him.

'Godamighty, I swear I didn't tell him nothin!' Benjamin T. Barlow pressed his back against the wagon, wishing he could push himself clean through it.

Two women had stepped from the concealing shadows of an alley, one a 'breed in a purple bodice and the other a redhead. A lion-cub look played on the 'breed's face as she came towards him, glare pinning him to the wagon. His heart palpitated, slamming at the inside of his ribs until he thought it might burst out. Sweat poured from his forehead and streamed down his face. He knew somehow who these women were, whom they worked for.

'You are not much on courage, Benjamin Barlow,' said the Indian girl, taking a step closer.

'Who are you? What do you want? I was just pullin' out.'

'I am called Wailai. Fala saw your wagon come into town and sent us to greet you, Benjamin. Imagine our surprise when we saw you talking to the marshal.'

A noise from the side caught his attention and he saw Julianka step from the back of her wagon and stop short as she spotted the two women. She started to turn but the redhead grabbed her arm and dragged her behind the wagon. Benjamin T. Barlow heard a stifled scream that was cut short by a sound he had once heard in a slaughter house, that of something cleaving into raw meat.

'Curious,' Wailai said, voice slow and measured, laced with Apache inflection. 'But when Ambrosia and I came through the alley, we overheard the strangest conversation. I think you are holding out on us, Benjamin. I do. I think you told Marshal Revere more than you would like to admit, more than you should have.' Benjamin Barlow shook his head violently in denial and seemed to shrink where he stood.

'I didn't tell him nothin', I swear I didn't. He said two folks got killed but I said I didn't know nothin' about them.'

'Oh, come now, Benjamin. You must do better than that. I was listening. You told him about the symbol and Fala's plans, did you not?' Wailai pulled her knife from her belt and his eyes bulged. Ambrosia stepped around the wagon, wiping blood on a portion of material torn from Julianka's dress.

'Oh, please don't do that! I didn't tell him nothin'!' Benjamin Barlow tried to press himself further into the wagon.

'You told him what we worship, didn't you, Benjamin? You told him about the shaman and Inkatani, the rise of the Apache warrior women.'

He could only shake his head in protest, voice locked in his throat. Wailai turned the knife blade to catch the rays of the early afternoon sun. The knife gleamed with dull light, sparkles of it flashing across his gaunt face.

'Fala always liked you, Benjamin. She told me so. If you tell me all you said I could put in a good word for you with her.'

'Y-you could?' Benjamin managed. His face brightened slightly.

'I promise, Benjamin.' Wailai pressed her body against his, a hand slipping over his bony shoulder.

'I, I just told him she was a powerful shaman, that's all. Didn't tell him nothin' else.'

'And what about Fala's plans?'

'Nothin', I didn't tell him nothin' about them, though he tried to make me. You heard, you heard what I said.'

'I heard most some of it. Are you sure you are telling me the truth? You wouldn't lie to Wailai, would you?' She pressed her lips to his, then pulled back.

'Nothin', I swear. He don't know nothin'.'

'That is most welcome news, Benjamin. Now I have to go. I cannot be late for school.'

'For school?' Benjamin mumbled, looking more relaxed.

'For school.' Wailai thrust the knife into Benjamin's ribs.

After watching the snake-oil salesman slump to the ground dead, Wailai turned to Ambrosia. 'Do you think the disgusting son of a pig was lying? I could not tell him I had come in on the conversation a lot later than he thought.'

'Reckon he was too plumb scared to lie,' said Ambrosia, looking smug.

'No one is too scared to lie.'

'What about Revere? Reckon he knows too much?'

Wailai stooped, yanked her knife out of Benjamin's chest and began sawing at his scalp. After she was finished she tucked the gory prize into her belt and wiped the bloody knife off on his shirt. 'We have to show Marshal Revere we are serious, that is all.'

'And if he still don't back off?'

'He will make a nice sacrifice to Inkatani.'

Billy Revere stepped from the school house, carrying his books and yawning. He'd had all he could do to stay

The Deadly Doves

awake in school today because he'd woken late last night to hear his ma and pa arguing again and it had kept him awake the rest of the night.

Billy hated it when they quarreled. Sometimes he wondered if it was his fault. Pa didn't seem happy and Ma was always away at the Hawkins place. He wished they had a real ranch, where his ma baked biscuits and pies and he helped Pa 'tend to raising horses or cattle like other kids.

Billy shook his head. He repositioned his books under his arm as other children rushed past him, hooting and hollering. The air smelled musky with fall and the chill didn't make him no nevermind so he let his coat swing open as he strode across the browning lawn and around the back towards the street, where he reckoned his ma would be waiting to pick him up.

He reached the opposite end of the schoolyard before he noticed two women leaning against a fence. They were dressed kinda strange. One, an Injun, he reckoned, wore a shiny purple top that showed more of a woman than Billy had ever seen. She had on a lot of warpaint, as his ma would call it, and looked like one of them women from the saloon he had heard other boys talk about: fallen women.

The other had on the same type of outfit and had red hair and eyes that looked too close together. They were both glancing at the various school kids, just the boys, he noticed.

Their gazes shifted to him and he suddenly recollected what his pa had told him this morning about being careful. He wasn't simple; he knew this must be what his pa meant.

The Indian woman gave him a look like she might want to scalp him and he began to pick up his pace. He had heard Pa and Ma arguing something about the saloon and he reckoned this might have something to do with it.

Billy, stepping up his pace another beat, didn't look back at first. Then a crawling sensation at the nape of his neck forced him to glance behind.

They were rushing towards him, almost running. 'Tarnation,' he muttered, heart drumming faster. He took a few more steps, looked back again, saw they were gaining.

'Oh-oh....' He broke into a full run, dropping one of his books. It fluttered to the ground in back of him and as he chanced another backward look he saw the women running, too.

Dashing around the plank fence that skirted the schoolyard, Billy sprinted across a back street and hit the boardwalk full speed. He scanned both sides of the street, hoping, praying to see his mother coming in the buckboard, but he knew she was sometimes late picking him up. The buckboard was nowhere in sight.

The women closed the distance, their strides longer, eating more ground, though Billy was faster than most of the kids at school. His heart jumped and his breath started to rasp out; his lungs set to aching as fear clamped his throat closed.

He ran faster, faster, faster, pumping his legs as hard as he could. But the doves – as he had heard his pa call them – were catching up. They'd overtake him any minute.

Billy's heart felt like bursting now. He pushed himself for more speed, but wasn't successful. His legs felt leaden, about to give out. He scrambled off the boardwalk and around the corner into an alley, veering around a stack of crates and a barrel. A sudden notion implementing itself before he could think about it, he flung the crates over behind him. The crates splintered as they hit the hardpacked ground. He scurried away as the women rounded the corner into the alley and stumbled around the obstacles, losing time.

'Ma!' Billy burst out as he came out of the alley on to the main street. He spotted the buckboard rattling down the rutted street and skidded to a stop. His mother jerked the reins and slowed the contraption and he leaped into the back, throwing his books in first.

'Billy!' a look of fright slapped Laura's face. 'What's wrong? What's happening?'

Billy, too out of breath to explain, jabbed a finger at the doves. They had stopped at the mouth of the alley, hesitating at the sight of the buckboard. They suddenly started forward again.

Laura's eyes narrowed. 'Who are they? What do they want?'

'Go-go-go!' Billy stammered. Laura snapped the reins and the buckboard shot forward, dust spewing up behind it. The Indian dove made a move to block its path, stepping on front of it, but dove away at the last second when Laura didn't bother to halt the horse.

NINE

Zach spent the rest of the afternoon looking through wanted posters and wiring a ranger friend for any information on Fala. He discovered nothing on her, but what Benjamin Barlow had told him about the woman gnawed at his mind. Barlow said she was loco, that she fancied herself a medicine woman who planned to build herself some sort of empire and return the Apaches to their former glory.

And seek revenge on the man who'd killed her mother.

The symbol was her brand, but why was it at the other saloons and on two bodies? Had she killed Whip and Sage? Zach saw it as likely, or perhaps she had someone else do it, maybe Hannely or Benedict, if they worked for her. But how could Zach prove it? And why would she kill one of her own girls and a no-good drunk gambler?

Hawkins....

Whip worked for Hawkins, but Sage, as far as Zach could see, had no connection to him. Did Fala? Had she left those bodies on Double H land for a reason? To frighten Hawkins? Was she somehow responsible for his missing stock? Was it all connected?

Zach reckoned it was, though he wasn't quite sure

how at this point. He had checked on Hawkins and the man's past was vague at best. The rancher had no active dodgers on him but his record seemed mired in murky trails that came to sudden dead ends and folks who'd no sooner talk about their dealings with him than a preacher man would reveal how much time he spent in a cat-house. A wagon full of greenbacks bought a lot of silence and like the sayin' went, deadmen told no tales.

He did know Hawkins had a reputation for being ruthless in his acquisition of land and crushing smaller outfits whom he saw as competition. Most of this went on through smoke screens he set up to keep his name dissociated from shady or merciless dealings while he carved himself a reputation as benefactor and slowly acquired half the holdings in town. By the time the railroad came through he might well be as big as Chisum, the cattle king.

Hawkins had also been working through Potter to put pressure on Zach about finding his rustlers and the more Zach thought about it the more he reckoned that pressure wasn't a fraction of what a man like Hawkins was capable of if he took the mind. He'd backed off completely on the bodies found on his land. Zach reckoned that was downright peculiar and it added to his suspicion and animosity for the man. It was almost as if Hawkins didn't really want things looked at too closely, like he was hiding something.

Zach knew Hawkins married late and had a small daughter. He treated the little girl like a queen, making sure she had the best of everything and had hired Laura to see to her learning. His wife had died in childbirth and as far as Zach could tell the marriage had been happy, though the woman had been more than half the rancher's sixty plus years. Hawkins had never been seen visiting any of the local saloons, though his men spent plenty of time there, so what possible connection would that give him to Fala or any of the owners, and why would any one of them steal his stock and leave bodies on his land?

Zach's reverie was snapped short as the door opened and the boy who had brought him the note from Calum burst into the office. The boy was out of breath from running and his eyes as big as hen's eggs.

'Marshal, you best come quick!'

Zach set his chair down on all four legs. 'What's wrong, son?'

'That wagon that come in to town . . .' The boy gasped between words.

Zach rose from his chair and slid into his coat. He set his hat atop his head. 'What about it, son? What happened?'

'That salesman and the gypsy, they plumb got themselfs kilt! Scalped, too! That reporter fella found 'em dead as corned beef jest a short spell ago.'

Zach's belly cinched and his face tightened. He knew suddenly Benjamin T. Barlow's magical elixir wouldn't be doing the man a galldamn bit of good from now on.

Benjamin T. Barlow didn't look good, but Zach reckoned he'd seen worse with Whip and Sage. The corpse was slumped beside the wagon and Bateman was standing over it, scribbling on his pad, an all too morbid excitement dancing in his eyes. Bateman looked up when Zach came up.

'Marshal Revere, we meet again.' His pencil stopped its track across the paper.

'You do seem to find your way around, Mr Bateman.'

'A good reporter tries to be where the news is, yessir, he does.'

'You found him?' Zach nodded to Barlow.

'Why, yes, yessir, I did. I was coming to try some of that magical elixir I had heard so much about. Appears my editor bought some and it cured his rheumatism immediately.'

Zach gave him a dubious expression and knelt, peering at the corpse. The man had been cleanly scalped and the knife wound was expertly placed above his heart. Zach patted the man's frock coat, coming across a pocket watch and a bottle of elixir, but no evidence of the greenbacks he'd seen the man stuff in his pockets. He uncapped that elixir and sniffed it, drawing back immediately. 'No wonder it cures rheumatism....' he muttered.

'How's that, Marshal?' Bateman asked, looking on intently.

'Reckon your editor'd get the same cure out of an Orchard bottle, Mr Bāteman, and it would taste a hell of a lot better.'

Bateman nodded, a thin smile on his lips. 'I would wager you're right, yessir, I would.'

Zach slipped the bottle back in Barlow's pocket and began unbuttoning the man's shirt.

Bateman got a puzzled look on his face. 'What are you doing?'

Zach didn't answer, merely finished unbuttoning Barlow's shirt and pulling it open. Blood had soaked the man's front but there were no other blemishes or wounds.

'Ain't here,' murmured Zach, peering at Benjamin Barlow's sallow-looking belly.

'What isn't?' Bateman asked.

'The brand that was on the other victims. That symbol.' Zach straightened and pointed to the one painted on the other wagon.

Bateman shrugged. 'So?'

'So nothing, I reckon.' Zach averted his gaze as Bateman's eye wandered.

'If you ask me, someone is doing us a favor, yessir, a favor. They'll clean up the riff-raff in this town long before you ever get around to it, Marshal. Hardcase gamblers, doves, snake-oil salesman and gypsies – streets might even be safe for decent folk again, yessir, safe. I plan to write that in my article for the *Tribune*.'

Zach gave him a sarcastic look. 'Sounds like vigilante talk, Bateman. You been makin' your own news?'

Bateman shook his head in disgust. 'I just write what I see, Marshal. I have no need to manufacture it, no sir, no need.'

'I thought that's what all you dime novelists did?'

Bateman scowled and Zach uttered a small laugh, then asked, 'Girl the same way?'

Bateman nodded. 'She's in the back of her wagon. Knife went right through her heart.'

'Reckon Julianka wasn't as good at lookin' into her own future as she was others.'

'Beg your pardon, Marshal?'

Zach shook his head. Benjamin T. Barlow and Julianka, he reckoned, had been unlucky enough to ride into the wrong town and wouldn't be selling snake oil or false futures ever again. Someone or ones had seen or overhead Zach talking to the salesman and Zach knew whoever it was had some connection to Fala and the murders, despite the lack of the brand on Barlow's body. It meant whoever it was was coming out into the open more and more, plucking obstacles from their path and delivering a message to Zach that he had better leave them be. He didn't need to be a gypsy to predict whatever future they planned would soon be unfolding.

*

'Hell, Hawk, how long you gonna let this go on?' asked Luis Fuego, Lockwood Hawkins's *segundo*. 'You lost blamed near enough cattle and horses to help someone start their own spread and you got two bodies dumped on Double H land.'

Hawkins turned from the bunkhouse window and eyed his *segundo*, a flash of fear in his eyes and a tightness in his belly. Luis had a point. He had let it go on too long, but Christamighty how could he have known she would track him down and set herself up in business in Carajo? She was just a girl when he last saw her; she could have been taken back by the Injuns for all he knew.

But he *had* known, maybe not when his stock first started disappearing, maybe not even after that man Foley was found on his land knifed and scalped. Hell, hardcase like that had more enemies than he could shake a stick at. Plumb likely any one of them could have killed him. Still something about the scalping had made him start to wonder, start to fear, and he had decided right there not to have that waste of a mayor Potter push the marshal on it too much. He had hoped it would just go away, though he reckoned in his soul he knew it would not.

Then came the girl. He had known instantly when they found the dead whore and he had seen the brand on her belly. A three-barred F. He reckoned that could only have belonged to one person and it was there as a warning to him that she was coming to claim her due. It had all come together after his *segundo* said he had seen the same mark at the Rusty Spur and other saloons in town. She was back. For him. Way she had screamed she would be. But, hell, he couldn't rightly kill a ten-year-old girl, could he? He had killed a handful of men without a second thought and that no-good Injun whore, but a little girl?

Even Lockwood Hawkins had his limits.

He knew from that point on it was merely a matter of time until she tried to do to him what she had done to Foley and that whore. And he had made sure the ranch house was well guarded and that he didn't go out at night or into town for a spell. His men were loyal to a fault – any one of them who wasn't would never get a chance to collect his severance pay – and he damn well couldn't bring the marshal into it, not without admitting Lockwood Hawkins was a murderer.

He sighed a weary sigh and his gaze settled on his *segundo* and the four other hands with him in the bunkhouse. He had called this meeting, galldamn tired of living with the fear and waiting for her to strike.

'Reckon you're right, Luis, and it's about time we did something about it.'

'What you plannin', boss?' asked one of the men seated at the long plank table. A lantern, turned low, spread buttery light and made the room shadowy as the sun sank behind the trees in the distance and dusk whispered over the land.

'I want six men, Luis,' he said looking back to his *segundo*. 'I want men armed with Smith & Wessons and no qualms 'bout killin'. Take them to the Rusty Spur and hang that woman who owns it.'

A collective gasp went through the men and Luis looked mildly shocked. His dark eyes narrowed. 'That's murder, Hawk. . . .'

Hawkins face went livid. 'Hell it is! That's justice! We're bringin' down a killer. We'll be doin' the town a favor and if I sit around waitin' she'll get me first.'

'What about the marshal, boss?' asked one of the men.

'Hell, he gets in the way kill him, too.'

'I don't want no part of this,' mumbled one of the men and Lockwood Hawkins's gaze went cold as it settled on him.

'I hear you right, son?'

The man seemed to shrink. 'Reckon I don't want no part of it. Ain't got the belly for no killin'.'

An unreadable look crossed the rancher's face. 'Well, hell, Cobsly, then you're free to go.'

The man looked slightly nervous, but stood and gathered his saddle-bags. Hawkins nodded to the *segundo* and said, 'Luis will take you to the house and give you a month's severance pay, Cobsly. Right nice workin' with ya and best of luck.' A coldness laced Hawkins's voice, but Cobsly seemed not to notice. The *segundo* led him outside and a moment of hushed silence fell in the room.

It was broken by the sound of a distant gunshot and the men exchanged nervous glances.

A few minutes later the bunkhouse door opened and Fuego stepped back inside. A man followed him in and Hawkins gave his second a questioning look. The *segundo* shook his head.

'Bateman! Glad you're here!' Hawkins put on a bravado to cover his fear and the worry the reporter might have seen what his second did with his disloyal hand.

'Your man told me you had some news for me, yessir, some news. I came right out.'

'Hell, Bateman since you're writin' up my life story and all I reckoned I'd make you privy to a bit of information you can put in your book.'

'Sir?' Bateman's gaze was questioning and Hawkins liked that. Bateman was gonna help him in his plan to be the biggest cattleman in the territory, was gonna make his reputation bigger than any of those gunfighters or other ranchers who ended up in dime novels.

'Tonight my boys are gonna go put an end to those murders. Won't be no more bodies showin' up on Double H land.'

Bateman's face tightened and a slightly worried look crossed his eyes. 'I don't think I understand.'

'I know who killed that hand and whore, Bateman, and I know it's 'cause she wants me dead, too.'

'She?'

'Yep, she. Woman owns a saloon in town.'

Bateman's face tightened another degree. 'Er, why would she want you dead or be killin' folks, Mr Hawkins?'

Hawkins felt his belly cinch. He couldn't come right out and tell the reporter the real reason, but he wanted to turn things to his advantage, build his reputation.

'She wants to take over my ranch, Bateman. She took this hankerin' for me and I turned her down. Now she thinks ruinin' me to get even will fix it.'

Bateman's eye wandered. Hawkins hated that. 'I don't see as how she'd go to so much trouble just for that.'

'Hell, Bateman, don't question me, just write it. The gal's plumb loco. You can see that just by the bodies she left.'

'What are you gonna do?'

'Why, my men are gonna round her up and hang her. Shoot her if she gives 'em any trouble comin' along. Make her an example for the town. By damn there'll be no lawlessness in Carajo. It'll be safe for decent folk.'

The look on Bateman's face wasn't quite what Hawkins hoped for but he didn't care. Bateman would write the story the way Hawkins dictated or else find himself another story – if he were alive to do it.

*

It was almost time.

Lockwood Hawkins stared out his parlor window, his mind tormented with thoughts of the past. She had found him, somehow, and tonight he was putting a stop to it.

Before she put a stop to him.

She would learn no one tasked Lockwood Hawkins. Her mama hadn't and she wouldn't, either. Hell, he would turn it his advantage, as he had done everything in his life. Though someone usually came out on the short end of his deals, he didn't care, never had. Others were put on earth to do his bidding, from that waste Potter to the marshal's wife, whom he rather fancied. He hoped the marshal did interfere tonight. If the lawdog were killed it would work out damn well for Lockwood Hawkins. He could step in and comfort Laura Revere, provide for her son and she would be eternally grateful.

He chuckled at the notion. Yes, he could see it quite well and it would make the perfect ending to Bateman's account of his life.

A sound.

Hawkins jerked from his thoughts, not sure at first he had heard anything at all.

It came again, a scraping sound, like a window being raised.

A quiver of fear went through him but he quickly passed it off. There were guards posted and at any moment Fuego would be riding out with the men to end the menace threatening him and the Double H. And there were servants – where the hell were they anyhow? He recollected he had dismissed them for the night.

The sound came again, followed by a soft laugh and he froze. He turned slowly and saw someone standing at the parlor entrance and for a moment he didn't dare move. Sallow lantern light fell on the figure of an Indian woman in a purple bodice. She looked like a 'breed of some sort and had an alluring smile on her lips and a lion-cub gleam in her eyes and for a moment he thought it was her, that she had somehow beaten him to the punch and come for him before his men could string her up.

Then he realized it wasn't her. This woman was young, barely out of her teens.

'Your guards are very inefficient, Mr Hawkins,' the girl said, smile growing wider. 'I easily disposed of the one circling the house. The rest of your men are occupied in the bunkhouse.'

'What the hell do you want?' He felt anger boil over the fear and took a step towards her. No galldamn little gal was gonna break into his house that way and expect to get away scott free.

'I want you, Mr Hawkins. Fala wants you. It is time.'

A jolt of fear hit him with the name. Fala. This girl had come from her. Well, if she thought he would make it easy for her she had another think coming. 'The hell it is. . . .' He dived for the Winchester on the parlor wall.

Another woman stepped from behind the foyer wall and blocked him. He made a grab for her, intending to throw her out of the way so he could reach the rifle. She sidestepped and something slammed into the side of his head, stunning him.

He staggered, didn't go down but whirled, a little off-balance. The 'breed had a Bowie knife in her hand and he knew she had hit him a glancing blow with the heavy handle. He tried to throw a punch at her but his body refused to work right. She laughed and swung the knife handle again. The thick handle collided with his temple and stars exploded before his vision. A third blow turned the stars to black.

'What's wrong?' asked Zach as his wife met him at the door. He shed his coat, tossing it on the hook.

'I want you to tell me what's goin' on, Zach.' Laura's face held a look of worry; not fear, but the next best thing.

His belly tightened and he hoped nothing betrayed itself on his face. 'What are you talking about?'

'Two "women" and I use the term very loosely, chased Billy after school today. If I hadn't arrived in time . . .'

'Godamighty. . . .' So they hadn't stopped with Barlow. They had decided Zach had gotten too much out of the snake-oil man and tried to do something about it, to his son.

'Is Billy all right?' Concern laced his voice.

'Yes, no thanks to you. Don't you think you'd better let me know what's goin' on before somethin' *does* happen?'

'Look, I want you to stay with your sister and her husband for a spell, get away from here.'

'Why? Who are these women? What do they want?'

'Lord's truth, I ain't sure. But it has somethin' to do with the murders of Whip Foley and that dove and Lockwood Hawkins.'

'Hawkins? How?'

'Reckon I haven't quite figured that out yet, though I got my suspicions. Whatever it is, they don't want me lookin' into it. Last night, when I came home, a note was stuck into the door with a knife; it said to leave them be.'

Laura looked incredulous. 'Why didn't you tell me? A knife in the door's a mite serious, don't you reckon? I could have kept Billy out of school today and stayed with him.'

'I didn't think they'd act on their threat. I didn't think they'd take the notion to do anything if I was careful. But a snake-oil salesman named Barlow was killed by them today. I reckon I was seen talkin' to him and they figure he gave me some information that could cause them trouble.'

Laura folded her arms, face serious. 'Zach, I realized when I married you there were risks involved, even though you gave up manhuntin'. I knew someone from your past might take a notion to get even for somethin' you didn't even recollect and I knew once you took the job of marshal that might happen as well. But you promised to be honest about it with me. Not tellin' me about a knife in the door and a threat to our family isn't bein' honest, not even close.'

Zach sighed. 'I reckon you're right; I should have told you. Maybe my judgement ain't been the best lately, but that don't change what happened. Now it's best to get you and Billy out of here.'

Laura let out a sigh. 'I don't want to leave, I don't want you goin' in there alone.'

'I got no choice, Laura. I can't let them keep murderin' folks and go ahead with whatever plan they got in mind.'

'Zach, you aren't a manhunter anymore, either. You just go in the way you use to you'll get killed.'

'I know I ain't, Laura. I reckon I'm startin' to realize that ghost that's been chasin' me might just be me lookin' for a reason for what I've become.'

Laura's eyes softened. 'Zach, what you've become is a father and husband if that's what you want to be.

That's your reason, that little boy in there who loves you, and me. I love you, Zach, and stay or go I don't want anything to happen to you. I don't even want you to be marshal anymore. I just want you makin' this ranch work for us and me contributing to that. If Hawkins is involved in this in any way then I won't go back to workin' for him and somehow we'll find another way to make ends meet.'

'Reckon Hawkins will have somethin' to say about that, Laura. Nothin' in Carajo goes on he don't want a hand in and you leavin' him high and dry to build somethin' he might see as competition won't set well.'

Her gaze dropped, came back up. 'I know, but we'll have to show him we're no threat and somehow come to a truce—'

Zach scoffed. 'Men like that don't cotton to truces. They devour everything in their path.'

'Zach, all I'm sayin' is that if you want to stay with me I'll compromise and we'll work it out together. But if your hankerin' to be what you were is so strong or you never truly decided to leave it behind then it won't work.'

Zach nodded slowly, a deep heaviness settling in his heart. 'I reckon you're right, Laura, and by damn I ain't a man who says I'm sorry easy but I'm sayin' it now. Maybe I wasn't ready to settle way I thought I was, maybe I ain't now. I just don't know at the moment. But I do know I can't risk anything happenin' to you or Billy – get your bag together.'

'Zach, please—'

'I ain't arguin' on it, Laura. I'll hitch up that buckboard you borrowed from Hawkins; that scalawag might as well be good for somethin'. You jest be ready by the time I come back for you.'

Laura started to give him a defiant look, but she

wound up heading down the hall to Billy's room. She knew from experience that when Zach's mind was set on something that was it.

He watched her go, the heaviness inside him growing worse. The ghost was here and he had to face it. There was no other way. But first he had to do something about Fala, find a way to bring her down. If he survived that he knew the ghost would no longer be chasing him.

It would be waiting.

As Laura pulled on the reins, bringing the buckboard to a stop in front of the small farmhouse belonging to her sister, Zach drew Gerty to a halt beside them. Billy rode in the back with the portmanteau. Rebecca Appleton's house was in Desmodeo, a nearby town, and Zach reckoned she and Billy would be safe there for the time being.

'Zach, please, I wish you'd reconsider.' Concern lay naked on Laura's face.

'You know I have to do this.' Zach's voice remained even but it was a struggle.

'Why, because it offers you a chance to break away from the daily routine you detest so much?'

He stared straight ahead into the night, the moon sparkling off leaves and dying grass coated with dew that would soon turn to frost. Shadows swayed as if each one were a menace, as if they had followed him here from Carajo to strike at his family.

His family . . . routine or not something inside him told him it was what mattered most to him and if it were taken away. . . .

He sighed. 'Laura, please, this isn't helping.'

Laura turned to Billy in the back. 'Billy, grab the bag

and go into the house. I want to talk to your pa a minute.'

Billy peered back, eyes vaguely frightened, as well as disappointed. 'Aw, Ma. . . .'

'Never mind "aw, Ma," – get in the house and tell your Aunt Becky I'll be in in a few minutes.'

Billy let out a sigh and hauled the portmanteau from the buckboard. Zach and Laura watched him disappear into the house.

Laura turned to Zach. 'I don't know where you got this death wish, Zach.'

'It's not a death wish. It's just somethin' I got to see through.'

'There's no discussing it with you, is there?'

'Reckon my mind's made up.'

Laura folded her arms and stared out at the dark countryside. Her lips cinched into a tight line. Then she climbed out of the buckboard and looked up at him. 'I'm not stupid, Zach. I smelled perfume on you when you came home last night. I don't know who she is but she'd better be worth it.'

Zach hoped the guilt he suddenly felt for his adulterous thoughts didn't mirror on his face. 'Laura, it ain't what you think.' Did that sound convincing? He wasn't sure.

'I love you, Zach, and I'll fight for you. But by God you better give me somethin' to fight for.' Laura whirled and hurried towards the house. He watched her vanish, then sat in silence for a long time, lost in his thoughts.

From the window, Laura watched Zach ride off, knowing what he was going to do could well get him killed. She had so worried lately that he would just decide to leave her and Billy, leave the security of their love for some foolish longing for what used to be. She couldn't compete with his ghosts, nor could she compete with some experienced dove practiced in the art of making men happy for short spells. She was what she was and loved him and that love came with responsibilities and a certain self-control that she wondered if Zach could commit to. She had sensed he meant that commitment when they first married, but things had changed some when Billy came and the responsibilities of owning a ranch and truly giving up the free life he had been used to had set in.

Did he love her enough for that? To give up the other women and freedom from attachments the trail offered? She prayed he did. But the decision had to be his and she would have to accept it either way.

But if he got himself killed that decision would be out of his hands. She couldn't let that happen.

Her sister had settled Billy into bed and Laura turned to her as she came from the short hallway. Rebecca was younger than her by three years but they had the same Appleton look and Laura's hair was only a hint darker.

'I have to go back out, Bec. Please make sure Billy's taken care of.'

Her sister appeared as if she were about to object but Laura knew the look of conviction on her own face stopped any protests.

Laura hurried outside and ran to the stable. She had unhitched the horse from the buckboard and had him saddled and ready to go. She guided the bay outside and mounted, gigging it into a good pace towards Carajo.

Half an hour later she approached the Mayor's office and drew up. She stared at the lighted window above the office, where she knew Potter maintained his living quarters.

Climbing from the saddle, she tethered the horse to the hitch rail and went to the office door, knocking. She banged two more times and when no one came she tried the handle. To her surprise the door was unlocked and she entered, looking over the darkened office.

'Mayor?' she yelled. 'Hello? Anyone here?'

Getting no reply she went to the back and started up the staircase. She took the steps without any attempt to be quiet and at the top she heard a giggle. She suddenly knew why the door was unlocked and a wry smile touched her lips. This might just work to her advantage.

She approached a door, hearing laughter and more giggles and grasped the glass knob. She stifled a laugh of her own and threw the door open.

A bleat came from the bounteously bare-bosomed dove perched beside the blanket-clad form of Mayor Potter, a candle in her hand poised over his chest. The dove set the candle on the nightstand and jerked the covers over her front.

'M-M-Mrs Revere!' Potter blurted, looking for all the world like a gal who just found out in full view of a room full of folks her skirt was stuck in her bloomers.

Laura grinned. 'Why, Mayor, I do believe I've caught you with your britches down. I think you can help me now. . . .'

The mayor looked suddenly as contrite as a man asking a preacher for pardoning for his sins. 'I reckon your wish is my command.'

The dove giggled.

TEN

The Rusty Spur was packed by the time Zach reached it. As he threaded his way through the sea of tables and boisterous patrons he scanned the room, spotting Fala behind the bar and myriad doves, some of whom were leaning on winners' shoulders, their bosoms spilling over their bodice tops, enticing them to exchange their monetary blessings for a more sinful type. He spied the 'breed dove and the redhead, who was warbling through *Bird in a Gilded Cage* on the stage, he had seen on previous visits. At the back, arms like fence logs folded across her massive front, stood the monstrous Indian dove. Zach noticed she was wearing a pair of man's boots and he reckoned he didn't have to ponder long just where she got them. But he knew their former owner was no longer in a position to object.

It was over tonight, he decided. He couldn't give them another chance at his family or let them kill again. The problem was he had no real proof or idea of just how extensive Fala's operation was. Did it include the other owners? Most likely. How many doves? Others? Zach wondered if he weren't just walking into the lion's den. He had to admit he had damn little in the way of a plan. In the old days he would merely have cornered the hardcase after isolating him. It would not be that easy with Fala and he had to be careful. He might have felt a longing for the old days but he had no death wish.

Zach's gaze stopped short as it fell upon the dark-haired girl heading around a table. She was wearing a blue sateen top that accentuated her cleavage and the ringlets in her hair bounced lightly as she walked.

'April. . . .' he mouthed. But she worked at the Golden Parasol. What was she doing here?

His palms went damp and a vague sinking feeling hit his belly. Before he could stop himself, he was in motion, angling towards her.

'Miss April,' he said, coming up behind her. She turned, recognition springing on to her face, but also something else: fear.

'Miss April, what are you doin' here?'

She gazed at him like a scared fawn. 'Please, Zach, I can't talk to you, they'll . . .'

'They'll what?' Anger began to trickle into his veins. This was something he hadn't expected, something that might alter his plans to confront Fala directly.

'No, I can't. I just can't.' April turned to walk away. He grabbed her arm and swung her around.

'Two doves made an attempt to get to my son today and I reckon Fala sent them. I got to know what's goin' on here and I have to stop it. I won't give them another chance at my family.'

'You're hurting me.' April tried to pull her arm free.

'Bothering the help, Marshal Revere? Or is this an official call?'

Zach turned to see Fala standing behind him. He tried to think fast. Although he had half considered confronting the owner with the few facts and the handful of supposition he had, April might provide him with better odds if she had more information.

'Strictly recreational. Reckoned I've had my fill of marshalin' for a spell and decided I'd give your place a try from the perspective of a customer instead of a lawman.'

'I'm sure, Marshal.' Fala's predatory gaze drilled him. 'What do you want with April, sugar? We got lots of girls here more experienced tendin' to a fella's needs.' Her question was direct, laced with challenge.

'I was just askin' this gal to spend a little time with me upstairs, but she seems a mite unwillin'.' He reached into his pocket and pulled out a double eagle. 'She's right pretty. I'm willin' to pay extra.'

'April, is that true?' Fala's gaze shifted to the dark-haired girl, daring her to make a mistake.

'Y-yes, I . . . didn't feel well and I reckon I don't like lawdogs.'

Fala's smile wasn't pleasant. 'You're workin', sugar. Marshal Revere is a payin' customer. I want you to be right nice to him. I reckon you're feeling much better now, ain't you?'

April's gaze dropped. 'Yes, ma'am.'

'Good. Then there's no problem.' Fala snatched the double eagle from Zach's hand. 'I reckon we should forgo your usual percentage until you can learn to be more sociable, don't you agree?'

'Yes, ma'am.' April's gaze remained fixed on the floor.

'There's an empty room right at the top of the stairs. Take the marshal up to it and make sure he gets his money's worth.' Fala pointed and smiled, no trace of magnanimity in her expression.

Fala departed for the bar and Zach took April's hand, guiding her towards the stairs at the rear of the room. They went up, the massive Indian dove's gaze stalking them.

The room was tiny with just a bare mattress and a small stand holding a lantern, flame turned low. He closed the door and looked at the frightened dove.

'What's goin' on?' he asked in a low voice.

Her eyes darted and she looked more frightened.

'You have to talk to me now. It's a sure bet Fala's involved in at least four killin's, and I reckon she won't be happy about the little stunt I just pulled.'

April stared back at him, eyes widening. 'I'm plumb scared,' she admitted. 'I didn't want to come here, Zach.'

'Why are you here instead of at the Parasol?'

'Juke sent me here. He said all the girls have to come here to be 'initiated'.'

'Initiated? Into what?'

'There's somethin' evil going on here, Zach. There's some kind of Injun cult. They make the girls take laudanum and opium pills or morphine syrup until they can't live without them.'

'Are you sure? Fala don't strike me as the type to bother much with that, least not as a main business. There's gotta be more involved.'

April nodded. 'The girls at the Parasol started comin' on strong after I left you the other night. I reckon one of 'em musta seen me talkin' to you. They said I h-ad to join. They said if I tried to run away they'd find me and. . . .'

'And what?' His suspicions, he realized, were all being corroborated by what April was telling him.

'That somethin' horrible would happen to me, somethin' like what happened to Sage and that gambler. They said Inkatani would take me.' A tear slid from April's eye and wandered down her face.

'Inkatani?' he asked, not sure what that meant.

'They worship him, Zach. Some sort of Injun devil.

They said he has to be appeased so the Apache women can rise again and take back what rightly belongs to the tribe.'

Zach grunted. He bet he knew what 'appeased' meant, if Foley and Sage were any indication.

'She's loco, Zach. She thinks she can take this town and every ranch in the area. And she's got some other plan but the girls wouldn't talk about that. I ain't sure they believe she's what she says she is, some kind of Injun witch, but they know she's dangerous and can do what she says she will, and they got no choice because she gets them addicted. Or she threatens to kill them.'

Zach nodded. 'I reckon she gets enough doves with her and money she might be able to pull it off but, there's only one way she'll have everything – she'll have to take it from Hawkins.'

'I don't like it here, Zach. I'm scared. I thought I could take care of myself, but I've never faced anything like this before. You've got to help me.' She pressed herself into his arms and tears dripped on to his shoulder. He held her, feeling awkward.

A knock stuttered on the door and April jumped back, a gasp escaping her lips. She peered at the door, fright in her eyes. It swung open and Zach turned towards it.

'I think your time is up, Marshal,' said the 'breed dove, stepping inside.

April, face bleaching, cast Zach a pleading look then hurried past the other dove and out the door.

Zach peered at the 'breed, who gave him a cold stare. 'Anything else I can get for you, Marshal Revere?' she asked, almost in a monotone.

'What's your name?'

'Wailai.'

The Deadly Doves

'Well, Wailai . . .' Zach pulled out another eagle. 'I'd like a little time with you.'

She tilted her head slightly, but the look behind her eyes could have frozen a side of beef. 'I take two of those for that. Can you afford me?' She gave him a forced practiced smile, dark eyes glittering.

'Reckon not, but I'll take it anyway.' He extracted another gold piece and handed them to her.

'You have determination, Marshal Revere.'

'Maybe. My wife has another word for it.'

Wailai pressed close to him, putting her hands on his shoulders, massaging them.

'Tell me about Inkatani,' Zach said.

'Very astute, Marshal Revere.' Wailai moved back and eyed him. 'You know more than we thought.'

'Do you worship him, too?'

She gave him a sly smile. 'What does it matter? My loyalty will be rewarded. My people will take back what is rightfully theirs.'

'What about Fala, will she take what she thinks is hers?'

'Ask her.' Wailai's words sounded cryptic. The hardness in her eyes solidified. 'How is your little boy, Marshal Revere? Well, I trust?'

It was Zach's turn to hide surprise. He hadn't expected her to come right out with it. 'Stay away from my family.'

'So all pretense is down, Marshal Revere? I thought so. There is a simple solution to our dilemma.'

'Drop my investigation?'

'Do not come here after tonight. Do not become involved any further. This does not concern you and we will be doing this town a favor by ridding it of . . . undesirables.'

'You're admitting to killing Whip, Sage and Barlow?'

'I am admitting nothing. This is merely some advice. Take it and your troubles are over; leave it and things could become much worse.'

'Aren't you afraid I'll hang you for murder?'

She laughed a lion-cub laugh. 'For what murder? There is nothing to prove. There is nothing you can do.'

Zach remained silent. She had him in a corner. He had no real proof and if he tried to bring in Fala no court would convict her, let alone hang her. He was limited by his badge.

'It would be best to concede the game, before it is over permanently.' Wailai forced the cold smile again and stepped towards the door.

Zach watched her walk out of the room. He came out behind her, seeing her go slowly down the stairs. Going to the landing rail, he saw her walk over to Fala and whisper something, then busy herself pouring drinks.

Fala glanced up at Zach, smiled, went back to polishing a glass. That smile said something. It told him what Wailai had said about him being left alone if he dropped his case was as far from the truth as it could get. They weren't about to let him walk out of this scot free. He knew too much, provable or not, to risk letting him interfere with their plans.

Fala did want to take control of the town and the surrounding ranches, set herself up as an Apache cattle queen, just as Barlow had said. Take over what her tribe had lost. But there would be more to it – a confrontation with Hawkins, whom she would have to oust in order to fulfill her plans. Hawkins was a powerful man and wouldn't take that sitting down and Fala knew it. Yet, Zach suddenly found himself thinking from what Barlow had told him, Fala might have another reason for going after the rancher. A much more personal reason.

His gaze went to the bar-room proper. The Rusty Spur had oddly begun to wind down and he bet the girls had been instructed to get the hands to drink up and leave with them. He saw a number of them filtering out with doves attached to their arms. Zach wondered if they weren't in for a night they wouldn't wake up from. Had Fala instructed a mass killing of Hawkins's men, as well as ones who worked for the other ranchers? Was her plan going into effect tonight, at this very moment?

Zach had a powerful notion it was.

He found himself in a quandary. He wasn't sure of his next move. Events and motives had fallen together in his mind, and he reckoned they weren't actually going to let him walk out of here, despite the pretense. That left him damn little option.

He edged towards the stairs, gaze locking on Fala, who averted her eyes when he looked over. She had been observing him, waiting for him to come down. So had Wailai. He gave the room the once over again, suddenly realizing April was nowhere in sight. His belly tightened.

He took the first step, hand absently sliding to his Peacemaker, feeling its comforting grip. He saw little choice but to draw it fast and aim his first bullet at Fala. Even if by some miracle they let him leave he was going nowhere without finding April and without fulfilling his duty.

A scream ripped from the back and he jolted, knowing that with that sound it had begun. The scream had come from somewhere beyond that door at the back of the room and he knew it belonged to April.

Zach's heart started to pound. He had made it halfway down the stairs and the burly Indian dove was barreling for the bottom of them at the first note of the scream.

As she reached the stairs he threw himself up and over the rail. He landed on his feet in the bar-room and bolted forward, crossing the room in three bounds.

The Apache woman moved with a speed Zach would have thought impossible for such a large woman. She managed to place herself between Zach and the rear door, looking for all the world like an enraged longhorn ready to charge.

The remaining doves started to scream obscenities and scramble around.

Zach scuttled sideways, trying to avoid the Apache, but was not entirely successful. The dove grabbed at Zach's coat, snatching a handful of the sleeve and using his momentum to hurl him around and back.

Zach slammed into a table hard enough to knock the breath from his lungs. Its legs buckled and the table collapsed, Zach crashing down on top of it. A cloud of sawdust billowed up. He shook his head, endeavoring to sweep away the sudden dust storm raging across his vision.

The mountain of a dove flung herself at him. Through blurry vision Zach saw the move in time to roll sideways and scramble back on heels and palms.

The dove tried to correct her plunge without success. Thunking down with a crash that sounded like a tree falling, she bellowed a screech and choice Apache words and immediately struggled to push herself up.

Zach gained his feet, and, chivalry aside, launched an awkward kick at the woman's ribs. It landed with a thud and the dove flew over, clutching her side and cussing in Apache.

Righting his balance, Zach pitched forward and jabbed another kick at the woman's face. The dove snapped out a beefy hand and snatched Zach's foot from mid-air, twisting.

Agony pierced Zach's ankle. He tried to turn with the twist, but lost his equilibrium and stumbled backwards, landing against another table. This one didn't give. Tumbling off, he crashed to the floor.

Zach cursed and attempted to get up, but the dove was already on her feet. She eyed him with a murderous glare, her lips drawn into a tight line and muscles knotted on either side of her jaw.

Managing to gain his feet before the dove could make another lunge, Zach shuffled forward, stopping in punching range of the mammoth Apache woman. The dove grinned. He threw a short chopping blow that cracked against the woman's jaw, snapping her head back, but doing little damage.

The blow was hard enough to drop any man, let alone a woman, but she merely stood there grinning at him.

He got little time to think about it.

The Apache dove grabbed two handfuls of Zach's coat and lifted him. Zach's feet left the floor and he was propelled backwards. He landed. Hard. Pain ripped through his back and the dust storm returned in his vision. A buzzing filled his brain.

The enormous dove grabbed him again, hoisting him up.

Zach's rattled brain recovered partially as the Indian readied for him for launching.

With all the force he could muster, the marshal brought both fists in short arcs against the woman's ears.

All expression dropped from the dove's face. She dropped Zach and clutched her head.

Zach stumbled backwards and fumbled for his

Peacemaker. Jerking it loose, he swung with all his might. The butt collided with the dove's temple. The burly woman froze; her whole body seemed to quiver. Then she collapsed, crumpling into a heap on the floor with a horrendous crash, groaning.

Already in motion, Zach holstered the Peacemaker and dashed for the back door. He snatched up the handle and threw open the door. A long hallway, almost pitch black, stretched out in front of him. He saw a dim light shining from the end of the corridor, and made for it. The light was coming from a room at the back and he knew that's where April would be.

A ruckus sounded behind him, doves yelling, Fala's husky voice cracking above the din, shouting orders.

Zach reached the end of the hall, hurled himself into the room without the caution all his years as a manhunter should have afforded him.

Two robed doves had April pinned to the floor. Her lip was swollen, bloody. Ugly welts and bruises crisscrossed her face. She struggled, but most of the fight seemed to have gone out of her.

Zach drew his Peacemaker. The girls, noticing him, released April and jumped to their feet. Each jerked a Bowie knife from her robe, flashing them menacingly and moving towards Zach. He swung the gun from girl to girl, in an effort to intimidate them, but the ruse failed.

One girl charged him, knife out-thrust. He sidestepped barely in time. The blade cleaved the air next to his face and he flinched. He tried to swing the gun up, but the second girl flung her knife and he had to dive to avoid it. The blade thucked into the wall just beyond where his head had been.

The first girl leaped at him again. Zach twisted, the knife swiping past his belly, slashing a chasm across his coat. He brought the Peacemaker's butt up in a vicious uppercut. It clacked against the girl's chin and snapped her head back. She crumpled into a heap at his feet.

The remaining girl made a dive for the knife embedded in the wall, wrapping her fingers around the handle. As she dived April managed to stick a foot in her way. The girl had the handle but she didn't have her balance. She went down, yanking the Bowie from the wall and rolling, then lay still.

Zach cautiously went over to her and poked at her sprawled form with a boot toe, discovering she had impaled herself on the blade. A puddle of red began to spread across the floor.

He had no time to dwell on it.

Rushing to April, who had pushed herself into a sitting position, he hauled her to her feet. 'Is there a back way out of here?'

'Down the hall to the left.' Her lips trembled and her face was ashen.

Zach guided her in that direction, circumspectly checking the dark hallway before leaving the room; it was deserted. A caution bell rang in Zach's mind. Why hadn't they come after him? Something struck him as too pat.

He had no time to dwell on that either. If they stayed in the room they would be trapped.

They hurried down the hall towards the rear exit, Zach in the lead, and burst through the back door, throwing caution aside in favor of expediency.

And stepped right into an ambush.

ELEVEN

The back door led into an alley littered with crates and barrels and dimly illuminated by the frosty light from a hanging lantern across the street.

Robed figures crowded the alley – the doves, each brandishing a Bowie knife or a derringer. The Apache dove Zach had knocked out led the pack, face bloodied and not at all amiable. A hatchet in hand, the big woman leaped forward as Zach and April came through the door.

Zach jerked his Peacemaker up, reflexively pumping off a shot.

Shock swept over the massive dove's features and her body jolted backward, stumbling a few mad steps before slamming with a huge thud into the hardpacked ground, dead.

'Don't!' shouted a husky voice, as Zach brought the Peacemaker around for another shot. He tensed, knowing he was outnumbered. Seven or eight doves, each armed, leveled weapons at him and April. Fala, dressed in a robe, stepped from the side shadows, holding an over-and-under aimed at Zach's forehead. The 'breed, Wailai, came up beside her, gaze centered on Zach.

'You can see the sense in not firing again, can't you, Marshal Revere?' Fala held his gaze, coppery eyes hard, dancing with an insane light. 'I can stand to lose Smells Like Buffalo...' she nodded at the massive dove's body. 'But I reckon I don't want to lose another one of my girls. I need them all, Marshal.'

'They're not all Indians...' Zach glanced at the doves. 'Most of them are white.'

Fala laughed. 'But they are in spirit, and Inkatani isn't particular about his followers. More importantly they are warriors, *women* warriors. Men have controlled the West for too long. Men destroyed my people, sent them to live in squalor and filth. It's time for a change.'

Zach remained still, gaze shifting to each dove, then back to Fala. She was right. It would be suicide to fire again. He could kill one, maybe two, three doves at the most, before a bullet found him.

'Your gun.' Fala motioned to Wailai. Zach lowered his weapon, handing it to the 'breed, who stashed it in her robe.

'Back up.' Fala gestured with her over-and-under.

Zach glanced at April, whose face was a mask of fear, then began to back up. The doves prodded them down the hall into the bar-room.

'Congratulations, Marshal Revere. You and April shall be privileged to something few mortals ever experience. You will be our sacrifices to Inkatani. You should be flattered.'

'Reckon you'll have to forgive me if I don't seem overjoyed,' Zach said, more with contempt than sarcasm.

Fala laughed without humor. 'Light the candles,' Fala commanded Wailai, who hurriedly complied by setting candles on tables. Striking a lucifer, she lit one then used it to set the others aglow. Flickering light gave the place an eerie atmosphere. Shadows fluttered like bats on the walls. One of the doves began to beat on a drum.

'Bring him,' Fala told Wailai when the girl was done lighting the candles. Wailai signaled Ambrosia and they went up the stairs, disappearing into one of the rooms above.

Zach's gaze shifted to the doves and Fala and he watched the proceedings with an odd feeling of detachment. He knew he was about to face his own death. In his years as a manhunter he faced death on every job, with every hardcase he tracked down. Somehow he had felt invincible in those days, as if it would never be him who tasted a bandit's lead, that he would always make the faster draw. In his mind, he suddenly saw the grief-stricken faces of his wife and son and felt afraid for them, not himself. A numbness filled his feelings and a mocking little voice in his mind kept saying, *You wanted a break from routine, wanted to relive the old days, well, now you have it. You'll never have to worry about routine again.*

'What now?' Zach asked.

'We wait,' said Fala.

'For Inkatani?' Zach asked caustically.

'Hardly. For the other members of our little . . .' she paused to meet the detective's gaze. 'Shall we say association.'

'Hannely and Benedict?'

'And some of their girls.'

'I thought you only wanted women?'

She laughed. 'Hannely and Benedict were useful to me. They had connections to the laudanum and morphine.'

'Were?' Zach raised an eyebrow.

Fala shrugged, keeping the gun aimed at him. 'They have the notion there'll be a place for them in my new order but I reckon they won't like it, so I am prepared to . . .' her expression darkened, 'cut them loose, as the cattlemen like to say.'

'This was all your idea? Your plan to – what? Become the biggest cattle owner in the territory? Reckon no one will cotton much to a woman runnin' things. Might find it hard to deal with some of those Associations.'

'They'll have little choice once everything belongs to me and is run by my girls.'

'And this little ceremony – you truly think some Injun god blesses your insane notions?'

'I am half Apache, Marshal. It is in my blood. Inkatani guides me, gives me strength and lets me see the future in visions. The day of the Apache warrior has come. We will be reborn tonight.'

'You're plumb loco.'

'Am I? I wish I could let you live to see how wrong you are, Marshal.'

'There's more to it, isn't there? More than just power and bringing the Apaches back to rule.'

'Barlow must have said more than Wailai and Ambrosia reckoned.'

'Enough, but he didn't tell me everything I needed to fill in all the pieces. But you did.'

'Did I? How so, Marshal?'

'By killin' a man who worked for the Double H spread, though that could have been coincidence.'

'It was not, Marshal. Whip Foley was just the man I needed to step up my campaign.'

'You stole Double H horses and cattle?'

She nodded. 'It was simple for an Indian. We sold them off at low prices to help us buy laudanum and morphine syrup. But many we have corralled miles from here. They were just to show the Double H we could do it, start the game of cat and mouse.'

'And with Foley you stepped up that game, decided to start putting the fear of Inkatani into the spread.'

Fala gave a short laugh. 'Very good, Marshal. You *have* been putting things together.'

'Reckon I don't understand killin' one of your own though.'

'Sage? Sage wasn't initiated. She didn't know of our plans and Inkatani and saw too much the night we killed Foley. I still could have turned her but she fit in nicely because I knew one man would see my brand and his fear would begin to tear him apart inside, make him know I was back and would take my revenge on him.'

'For killing your mother. . . .'

The insanity in Fala's eyes intensified. 'That's right, Marshal. He must pay for that, slowly. I will brand him alive and take his scalp while he screams for mercy. I will watch him suffer as he made her suffer. And then I will kill him and take all that is his.'

Sounds of a struggle and a loud voice came from the top of the stairs and Zach looked up to see Wailai and Ambrosia pulling a man towards the steps. The man's arms were bound behind his back and his face was twisted with fear. He struggled harder and they had a hard time holding him.

Wailai drew a Bowie knife from beneath her robe and jammed it to his ear, threatening to cut it off if he didn't comply with their demand to descend the stairs. He ceased struggling and came down. They brought him up to Fala, whose gaze fell on him with utter contempt and fury.

The man looked at Zach. 'Cristamighty, Marshal, do

somethin'. These women are loco.' Spittle formed at the corners of Hawkins's mouth and tears were running down his face.

Fala looked at Zach. 'Have you guessed, Marshal?'

Zach nodded. 'He killed your mother.'

'These whores are loco, Marshal. Galldamn loco! I never killed no one!' Hawkins's voice was deteriorating, getting shaky, choked with fear. 'I'll pay you anything, Marshal. You gotta stop 'em.'

'The marshal's hardly in a position to stop anybody, Hawkins. He'll die after you do, and you'll die slowly, indeed. You murdered my mother and went about your life as if it had never happened, as if no one cared because she was just an Indian, an Indian whore. But I cared, Lockwood Hawkins, and I waited, gaining all the power of a shaman, filling myself with the blessings of Inkatani. Now you will taste my knife and I will show you the same mercy you showed her.' When Fala nudged her head, Wailai and Ambrosia pushed Hawkins back. He began to blubber as they forced him on to a table and motioned for four doves to come over and hold him down.

Wailai and Ambrosia moved closer to Zach and April, the redhead pushing April away from Zach a few paces and holding a derringer on her.

A commotion sounded from the doors and Zach's gaze shifted to see Juke Benedict and Morgan Hannely entering, followed by a dozen derringer-armed doves. Benedict and Hannely carried Smith & Wesson's and Zach saw Fala cast them a glance.

'Looks like everyone's here for your little shindig—' Zach froze. Another figure had stepped through the door, one that he recognized with a sinking feeling of dread. The man came up to him, left eye wandering as his gaze centered on Zach.

'You should have left things alone, Marshal. A drunk, a whore, a snake-oil salesman – who would have cared in the grand scheme of things?'

Zach scoffed. 'I should have known, Bateman. Fala needed someone to stick close to Hawkins and tell her everything he was thinking, his reactions. I hope you got paid enough to throw away your integrity.'

Bateman laughed. 'I will be. My *real* story, Marshal, unique and the biggest sensation of all time, how a woman became cattle queen of New Mex and brought the Injuns into the modern age.'

Zach scoffed. 'The world ain't ready for that. Even if they accept a woman runnin' a huge outfit they won't accept an Indian. You know it as well as I do.'

'You're wrong, Marshal,' said Bateman. 'Fala will own everything. They'll have no choice but to deal with her and respect what she is.'

'Respect ain't stolen, Mr Bateman. And I reckon the government might just see it different. You ain't thought this through.'

'Reckon once I glorify it in my novel the world will be convinced. The power of the pen, yessir, the power of the pen. Mr Hawkins was plannin' on using me to spread his name, make him bigger than Chisum. It'll work the same for Fala, you mark my word, yessir, my word.'

'You're as loco as her.' He ducked his head at Fala.

'Remove his shirt!' Fala suddenly shouted to Ambrosia, jutting a finger at Hawkins, who let out a bleat of terror. Ambrosia moved to the table and swapped her derringer for a Bowie knife beneath her robe. She began to cut away Hawkins's shirt.

Wailai went to the pot-bellied stove, withdrew a branding iron that glowed orange and came back towards the table.

The Deadly Doves

'After we kill him, Marshal Revere will have the pleasure of watching April be sacrificed to Inkatani.'

April let out a gasp and looked pleadingly at Zach.

Zach knew he was going to die. There wasn't much question about it. But the method, he reckoned, was one he had some control over. He could watch them kill Hawkins and April and perform some brutal Indian ceremony, let them take over the town and all the local spreads, or he could fight his way out, go down with dignity, as he would have as a manhunter.

Wasn't much of a galldamn choice, he reckoned.

Wailai made a move towards Hawkins, as Ambrosia finished cutting his shirt away. She raised the branding iron then pressed it against the rancher's bare belly. A harsh sizzling and searing filled the area with the stench of burning flesh.

But when Wailai moved to Hawkins she placed her back between Zach and Fala, making a direct shot at him with the over-and-under a more difficult proposition.

It was a huge risk but Zach took it. He moved, lunging forward and thrusting his arm out sideways. It collided with April, propelling her diagonally toward the door leading to the back area.

She went through the opening, stumbling and falling in the hallway that led to the back room, but out of immediate danger.

In nearly the same move, Zach grabbed for Wailai, who stood momentarily startled, frozen. He got his left arm around her throat and jerked her close. Shoving his free hand into her robe, he located his Peacemaker. He swung Wailai around, using her as a shield between himself and Fala.

'Come now, Marshal Revere.' Fala raised her gun. 'Do you think I'd let the life of one follower prevent me from stopping your escape and ruining all my plans?' She fired. Zach was shocked at the sudden, unexpected callousness of the move. He thought he had a bargaining chip, a moment of negotiation. Now he held a corpse, having all he could do to keep his balance under the impact of the slug plowing into Wailai's chest.

Fala adjusted her aim for another shot, higher, at his unprotected head.

He flung Wailai's body from him. She couldn't have weighed more than a hundred pounds but she was still dead weight in more ways than one. She flopped forward like a ragdoll as Fala fired a second time. Another bullet plowed into the 'breed; her body jerked and crumpled.

Zach twisted, hurling himself backwards over the small stage before Juke and Hannely managed to recover enough composure to start blasting with their Smith & Wessons or for the other doves to fire their derringers or use their knives.

He reared up suddenly. Bullets whined and spanged from the stage around him, gouging out chunks of wood and sending splinters flying, as some of the doves fired hastily and the other two owners triggered shots. He knew the stage would afford him little protection under such a volley and fired back.

Hawkins shrieked in terror on the table. The doves holding him let go and dived for cover, firing derringers. The rancher rolled off the table, hands still bound behind his back and Zach caught a glimpse of him trying to get to his feet.

Fala thrust a hand into her robe and brought out a Bowie knife, hurling it at Zach in nearly the same move. The blade splintered the edge of the stage. She hadn't expected him to spring up like a jack-in-the-box and present himself as a target and had hurried her throw, aimed low.

He jerked his Peacemaker up, squeezed the trigger. The gun blasted and a look of shock froze on the woman's face. She flew backwards, a bullet hole in her chest gouting blood.

The other owners scrambled for the meager cover of the tables. Bateman dived behind the bar before Zach could get a shot at him and came up with a scattergun.

The front doors burst open and more men charged into the saloon. Zach wasn't sure at first who they were, then saw three of the men who had been with Hawkins at the scene of Whip and Sage's bodies and three others. His hands. Zach put it together in a flash of understanding. Hawkins had realized Fala was out to get him and planned accordingly. He had set in motion a plan to attack her first but her doves had managed to kidnap him before it happened. Zach bet Bateman had something to do with informing her of the rancher's plans.

The men made it inside, firing randomly. Doves screamed, bullets finding them and sending them over tables and crumpling to the floor, dead.

Hannely and Benedict turned and started firing at the hands. One of Hawkins's men went down and another aimed at Hannely, putting a bullet through the saloon owner's heart. Five others took aim on various doves and Benedict sent a bullet at another of Hawkins's men, killing him instantly.

Zach swung his Peacemaker on Benedict and triggered a shot that sent the saloon owner reeling, stumbling backward over a chair and crashing to the sawdust, dead.

Blood splattered and sawdust flew up. Screams and

gunfire filled the room and blue smoke drifted in thick clouds.

Another of Hawkins's men went down from a dove burying a Bowie knife in his back, and one of the remaining three blasted a shot that sent her small body half-way across the room.

Zach kept firing, plucking shooting doves from their concealment.

Bateman took aim on Zach and triggered both barrels of the scatter-gun, but the reporter's aim was hasty and poorly directed. Zach dived and got out of the way but one of Hawkins's men did not. The shot tore him into a bloody mess and dropped him instantly.

Hawkins's other two men swung on Bateman, unsure exactly whether the reporter had betrayed them or merely mis-aimed. They fired at nearly the same time and Bateman took a backward leap into a hutch filled with whiskey bottles. The bottles rained on him as he slid to the floor, some exploding as errant bullets plowed into them.

Zach knew it was nearly over. Doves were trying to run more than fight now and he felt a sudden burst of confidence.

But the confidence was quickly dashed as Hawkins, miraculously unhit, got to his feet and bellowed at his men: 'Kill him!' He nudged his head at Zach.

Shocked, Zach swung towards the men on pure instinct for survival. His reflexes might have slowed but enough speed and accuracy remained.

He fired just as one of Hawkins's men swung his aim at Zach's head. The man jerked a shot after Zach's bullet punched into his chest, but it plowed harmlessly into the floorboards.

The other hesitated and Hawkins yelled: 'Kill him, for chrissakes, Fuego!'

The Deadly Doves   155

Fuego raised his gun and Zach tried to fire first. The hammer fell with an empty *clack* and his belly sank. He was out of bullets and had no chance in Hades of reloading. The man had him.

As a shot blasted, Zach braced himself for the bullet.

It never came.

A blank expression crossed the man named Fuego's face and he pitched forward, gun blasting as he fell, bullet burying itself in the floor.

Behind stood Deputy Jesse James Buchanan, his Peacemaker smoking.

A hush fell over the saloon. Clouds of blue smoke drifted by and the hollowness of death settled in the room. Any of the doves whose bodies weren't sprawled on the floor had run and Zach reckoned that was the last he'd see of them.

Zach looked at Hawkins, who suddenly had fear back in his eyes. Slowly he plucked bullets from his gunbelt and reloaded his Peacemaker, then walked over to Hawkins. He placed the gun barrel to Hawkins forehead and the man began to whimper, dropping to his knees.

'P-please, Marshal. . . .'

'You didn't plan to show me any mercy, Hawkins. All your money won't buy you out of this. You're a killer.'

Hawkins eyes darted back and forth in their sockets and tears streamed down his face. Lockwood Hawkins was a coward a heart. He killed defenseless women or had others do his dirty work.

Zach withdrew the Peacemaker and stepped around Hawkins. He grabbed the man's bound arms and hoisted him into a chair, then flipped a table on to its legs before the rancher. Hawkins watched, fear and confusion in his eyes.

Zach found a Bowie knife on one of the dead doves

and went behind Hawkins, slicing his bonds. Plucking a Smith & Wesson from Hannely's dead fingers, he checked the chamber, finding two bullets left.

Going over to the table he sat in the chair opposite Hawkins and placed the gun in front of the rancher on the table. Then Zach set his own Peacemaker on the table and withdrew his hand.

His gaze met the rancher's. 'Used to give my quarry a choice, Hawkins. Sometimes I knew the law wouldn't convict them because I had no proof. But I did have a license to kill. I let them make the decision themselves; they could either sign a confession and hang for their crimes or take the chance they could beat me to the draw. I'm givin' you that choice. You confess right here and now in front of the deputy and me or go for that gun in front of you . . .'

'Hell I will! You'll just gun me down if I go for that.'

'Then confess.'

'You're loco! I ain't gonna hang.'

Zach's gaze held his and sweat dripped down the man's face. 'You're a coward, Hawkins, and you got no choice. You killed a woman and had your men come to do your dirty work tonight. Now you got a chance do it yourself this time. You might beat me if you go for that gun, or redeem yourself if you confess.'

Hawkins's gaze flicked from Zach to the Smith & Wesson before him, then back again. His lower lip started to quiver.

A beat. Two.

It came then. He saw it flash in Hawkins's eyes. The man would never confess and face hanging. It was not in his nature.

Hawkins's hand slapped for the Smith & Wesson. Zach's hand was in motion the same instant, going for the Peacemaker.

Hawkins plucked the gun from the table, jerked it up.

Zach's fingers wrapped around the Peacemaker's grip and he brought it to aim, fired.

Hawkins's face turned with shock and he went backwards, chair and all. He hit the ground with a thud and didn't move, a hole in his forehead.

Zach didn't move for a moment. The ringing of the gunshot faded in his ears and he felt little sense of satisfaction with Hawkins dead. Maybe it had been too easy a solution to kill the man, though he certainly deserved worse than the chance Zach had provided him. It would not, however, solve all his problems, nor vanquish the ghost.

He looked up at Buchanan, who nodded. 'How'd you know?'

'You can thank your wife. She rousted Potter into fetchin' me.'

'How the hell did she do that?'

Buchanan shrugged. 'Don't know, but he was 'bout fallin' over himself tryin' to help her.'

A sound came from behind them and Zach turned to see April coming from the back. Buchanan swung his gun to her.

'She one of them?' he asked.

Zach stood, shaking his head. 'She helped me and they tried to kill her.'

April ran to him and he held her as she cried. Buchanan holstered his gun. 'I best get the 'taker out of bed, too. He's got a lot of business comin' his way.'

'Tell him Hawkins will pay for it.'

'What will you do, April?' Zach asked, drawing Gerty to a stop in front of the boarding-house.

April climbed from the saddle and looked up at him,

residual fear still lacing her eyes. 'Ain't sure. But I'm done workin' in the saloons. Maybe I'll go East, go to school. I've seen too much death.'

So had Zach and it didn't settle well. Maybe that had been the biggest change in him, the signal he had been waiting for. 'It'd be a hell of a lot safer. And you probably won't run into any self-proclaimed shamans there.' Zach winked, a thin smile on his lips.

'Reckon maybe I could get some of my self-respect back? I've come to realize I've been missing it lately.'

'Reckon you already have it, then.'

She paused, then gave him a pleading look. 'Come in, Zach. Please. You can spend the night. After all that's happened tonight . . . I could use a little companionship. I think you could too.'

Zach sighed. He still felt strongly attracted to her and it showed, but something inside him had changed and he wasn't quite sure what. Knowing Billy and Laura were in danger, maybe, or perhaps something deeper than that. 'I've got a lot of things I ain't satisfied with. But when I look deep inside, I begin to think what I got is a lot better than what I could trade it for. I don't belong on the trail anymore and hell, maybe I don't even belong bein' marshal. Maybe I needed tonight to show me that those days are truly gone.' He looked forward, gaze searching the night for nothing in particular, then back to her. 'I love my wife, April, maybe even my routine. I ain't willin' to throw it away.' He paused. 'If it's any comfort, you would have been the one I might have thrown it away for.'

'You're a nice man, Marshal Revere. A really nice man.' April turned, starting up the walkway, then stopped and looked back at him. 'Too bad.' She smiled then went towards the boarding-house.

Zach watched her go inside and let out a little laugh

that might have been the closest thing to satisfaction he'd felt in years. He gigged Gerty into motion, for once actually looking forward to getting back to his routine.